Amish Homecoming

Jo Ann Brown

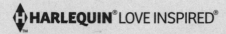

Recycling programs
for this product may
not exist in your area.

LOVE INSPIRED BOOKS

ISBN-13: 978-0-373-71928-0

Amish Homecoming

www.Harlequin.com

Printed in U.S.A.

Arise; for this matter belongeth unto thee: we also will be with thee: be of good courage, and do it.
—*Ezra* 10:4

To Bill
my "city boy"

Chapter One

Paradise Springs
Lancaster County, Pennsylvania

"I can't believe my eyes. Is that who I think it is?"

Ezra Stoltzfus looked up from the new buggy he'd been admiring. His older brother Joshua had done an excellent job with the courting buggy he was building for his son. It was low and sleek, exactly what Ezra's nephew Timothy would want when he was ready to ask a special girl to let him take her home from a singing.

He was about to ask Joshua what he was talking about, but then he looked through the large glass window at the front of his brother's buggy shop in the small village of Paradise Springs. Every word fled from his mind.

It couldn't be. Not after all this time. It had been ten years.

Getting out of a family buggy in the parking lot of the line of shops connected to the Stoltzfus Market was a slender woman dressed plain in dark purple. From beneath her black bonnet, her white *kapp* peeked out along with her golden hair that glistened in the spring sunshine.

A small, black dog jumped from the buggy and stayed close to the woman as she spoke to someone inside. She smiled, and he knew.

It *was* Leah Beiler!

He couldn't have forgotten Leah's heart-shaped face with the single dimple in her left cheek. Not if he tried, and the *gut* Lord knew how much he'd tried for the past ten years, since she and her twin brother, Johnny, left Paradise Springs. They'd gone without telling anyone where they intended to go. They hadn't come back.

Until today.

Did her family know she was back? They must, because she was driving Abram Beiler's family buggy. He recognized it by the dent where his neighbor had scraped a tree on an icy morning a few months ago and hadn't gotten around to bringing it in to Joshua to get it repaired. Why hadn't Leah's *daed* mentioned that his *kinder* were home? They'd spoken three days ago when Abram came over during milking to talk about the selection of a new minister for the district at the service on the next church Sunday. Abram had mentioned he was going to be away at a horse and stock auction west of Harrisburg for over a week and that he hoped he'd be home in time for calving, because several of his cows were due to deliver soon. How could Abram have talked of those commonplace things and never mentioned his twins had come back after so many years away?

Ezra couldn't forget the conversation he and Abram had the very day Leah and Johnny had disappeared. They'd spoken about Abram's youngest daughter, who was torn between her love for her way of life and faith in Paradise Springs and her twin brother's increasing rebellion against both, as well as his family.

Ezra had reminded Abram of Leah's strong faith and her love for her family, but he understood her *daed*'s concern. She was always determined to rescue any creature needing help. It didn't matter if it was a baby bird fallen from its nest or her wayward brother who kept extending his *rumspringa* rather than committing to his community and God. She would throw everything aside—even *gut* sense—if she thought she could help someone. It had been her most annoying quality, as well as her most endearing. He knew of her generous heart firsthand because Leah had been there for him during the months when he grieved after his beloved *grossmammi* died…and many other times for as long as he could remember.

That day, as they talked on the Beilers' porch, Abram had been at his wit's end with worry about his youngest *kinder*. Otherwise, he never would have admitted to his concerns. Abram Beiler was a man who kept his thoughts and feelings to himself.

Was that why Abram hadn't said anything the other day? Ezra didn't know how a man could keep such glad tidings to himself…unless the tidings weren't *gut*. Could it be Leah and Johnny hadn't really come home to stay?

Ezra looked around the parking lot in front of the Stoltzfus Market. He saw a few cars and a couple of buggies, but no sign of Johnny. Was he in the store, or was he still in the buggy? When Leah smiled again as she spoke to someone in the buggy, he wondered with whom she was chatting. Her brother? A husband? A *kind*?

His gut crunched as the last two questions shot through his mind. The whole time Leah had been gone, she'd remained, in his mind, that seventeen-year-old girl who was always laughing and who always had time to listen to his dreams of running his family's farm and starting his own cheese-making business. Oddly enough, she was the only one who hadn't laughed at his hopes for the future.

Now she was back in Paradise Springs and at the shops run by his brothers. Where had she been and why had she come back now?

Joshua set down his hammer as he turned to Ezra, his mouth straight above his dark brown beard. "I guess I don't have to ask. The expression on your face says that it's got to be Leah Beiler."

"The woman does look like her, but she's turned away so I can't be completely sure." He kept his voice indifferent as he walked from the window toward the table where Joshua kept paperwork for new buggies and repairs on used ones, but his older brother knew him too well to be fooled.

"Even so, you think that's Leah Beiler out there."

He nodded reluctantly. The last time he had been false with Joshua was when they both were in school and Ezra had switched their lunch pails so he could have the bigger piece of their *grossmammi*'s peach pie. His reward had been a stomachache and an angry brother and a *grossmammi* who was disappointed in him. At that point, he had decided honesty truly was the best way to live his life.

So why was he lying to himself now as he tried to convince himself the woman could not possibly be Leah?

"Are you going to talk to her?" Joshua asked as he glanced up at Ezra, who was four inches taller than he was. Joshua was the shortest of the Stoltzfus brothers, but stood almost six feet tall. A widower for the past four years, he had the responsibility for three *kinder* as well as the buggy shop.

"I wasn't planning on it." He stared at the neat arrangement of tools on the wall so he didn't have to look at his brother…or give in to the temptation to glance out the window again.

"You're not curious why they went away?"

He wanted to say he wasn't any longer. Not after ten years. But that would be a lie. At first, after she and Johnny vanished, he had thought about Leah all the time. She'd been such an important part of his life, around every day because they'd grown up on farms next door to each other.

Then, as time went on, he found himself thinking of her less because he was busy taking over the farm from his *daed*. Chasing his dreams to become a cheese-maker consumed him, allowing him to push other thoughts aside. Yet, he'd never forgotten her. At night, when the only sounds were his brothers' snoring and the crackle of wood falling apart in the stove, memories of her emerged like timid rabbits from under a bush. They scampered through his mind before vanishing again.

And always he was left with the questions of why she had left and where she had gone and why she'd never returned.

"Of course, I'm curious," Ezra said before his brother noticed how he hesitated on his answer.

"Then go out and see if she's really Leah Beiler." Joshua gave him a sympathetic smile. "You'll kick yourself if you don't."

His brother was right, and Ezra knew it. After spending too many years on "if only," he could not add another to his long list of regrets. God had brought this unexpected opportunity into his life, and ten years of prayer for an explanation could be answered now.

"All right." He took his straw hat off a peg by the door and put it on his head.

"Then let me know," Joshua called to his back. "You're not the only one who's been wondering if we'll ever know the truth of why she and Johnny left. And why they're back."

Ezra nodded again as he opened the door. Fresh spring air flavored with mud and the first greenery of the season filled the deep breath he took while he walked out of Joshua's buggy shop and into the midmorning sunshine. It took every ounce of his willpower to propel his feet across the parking lot toward where Leah stood by the buggy.

The crunch of gravel beneath his work boots must have alerted her, because she glanced over her shoulder toward him. Surprise, mixed with both pleasure and uncertainty, widened her eyes. They were the same warm shade as her purple dress, and that color had fascinated him since they were young *kinder*. Like her dimple, they had not changed, but she seemed tinier and more fragile. An illusion, he knew, because he had grown taller since the last time they were together. In addition, Leah Beiler was one of the strongest people he had ever met, the first to raise her hand to volunteer.

"*Gute mariye*, Leah," he said quietly as he stepped around the small dog who ran from her to him and back. So many times he had imagined their reunion and what he would say when he saw her again. He couldn't recall any of it now when he paused an arm's length from her. The memory of the girl she had been, which had become flat and dull through the years, dimmed further as he beheld the living, breathing woman in front of him.

"Good morning," she replied in English, then repeated

the words in *Deitsch*, the language spoken by the Amish. She acted unused to it now. "How are you, Ezra? You look well."

"I am. You?"

"I am fine." She glanced along the storefronts in the small plaza with the market in the middle. A simple sign by the road stated Stoltzfus Family Shops. "Are all these businesses owned by your family?"

"Ja." He pointed to each shop as he added, "Joshua builds buggies. Amos owns the market. Jeremiah and Daniel are woodworkers, and Micah makes windmills. Since the bishop approved us using solar panels, he's been installing them, too."

"What about Isaiah?"

"He has become a blacksmith, and his smithy is around back." He wondered how she could act as if everything were normal, as if she and Johnny had not disappeared abruptly.

"Leah?" asked a sleepy voice before he could blurt out the questions swirling through his head.

She turned to look into the carriage. He did, too, and saw a girl sitting in the buggy, a girl who looked like Leah had when he and she were both going to school together.

He knew at that instant nothing could be the same as it had been before she left.

Leah Beiler had known the chances were *gut* that she'd see at least one of the other Stoltzfus brothers when she came to speak with Amos Stoltzfus at his market, but she hadn't expected it would be Ezra. She'd hoped for more time before she spoke with him, more time to become accustomed to the plain life she had left behind a decade ago. Even though she'd tried to stay true to the ways in which she had been raised, some *Englisch* ways, like looking for a light switch when it was dark, had subtly become habits she needed to break.

At least the propane stove seemed familiar this morning when she rose to make breakfast, because she had used a gas stove the whole time she was away from home. Johnny had suggested an electric one, but she'd refused, one of the few times she'd put her foot down after they left Paradise Springs.

She was glad for the excuse to look away from Ezra when Shep gave a yip as another buggy pulled into the parking lot. Calming the dog, she tried to do the same for herself. She had offered to come to the market to get some cinnamon for *Mamm* because she had wanted to speak to Amos about displaying some of her quilts for sale. The quilts she had made and sold during the past ten years provided money to feed and shelter them, and she hoped she could go on selling them to help with expenses at home now that her parents were older. She had been thinking of that instead of realizing she shouldn't have come to the market without preparing herself for a chance encounter with people she'd known.

Especially, she should have thought about the possibility of running into Ezra. Time had turned the awkward teen with limbs too loose and long for him into a handsome man. He had definitely grown into himself, because his suspenders seemed narrow on his wide shoulders and muscles were visible beneath his rolled-up sleeves.

He didn't have a beard, which meant he'd never married. That surprised her because several of the girls who had been her friends before she left Paradise Springs had talked endlessly about Ezra Stoltzfus. At the time, he'd seemed oblivious to their hopes that he would ask to take them home on a Sunday after church. He was kind and teased them, but, if he agreed to take one of them home, it was because he was going to see one of their brothers and wanted to be polite. She had been certain he would ask Mary Beachy to walk out with him…until the night he kissed *her*.

Did he remember that night? They had been sitting by the stream that cut through the back fields of her family's farm, and he'd leaned over to shoo a mosquito away. She had turned her face to thank him, not realizing his was close. Their lips brushed. The kiss had been swift, but the reaction had remained with her all night as she recalled how warm his mouth had been against hers.

She never had a chance to ask him if he'd meant the kiss or if it had been an accident. The next night, Johnny had the worst argument ever with their *daed* and left, taking her with him. He'd offered to go with her into the village for an ice-cream cone. Instead, they met a young woman in a car. Johnny had insisted Leah come with him when he got into the car. She'd gone, knowing someone had to try to talk him out of his foolish plan.

For ten years, she'd repeated the same plea for him to return to Paradise Springs and their family and their home and their friends. Not once had he wavered. He would not go back to their *daed*'s house.

And he had been true to his word.

But she had come home…at last. Her hope that it would feel as if she'd never been away was futile. Ten years of living among *Englischers* had altered her in ways she couldn't have foreseen. Now she had to relearn to live an Amish life.

And her niece Mandy must learn to live one for the

first time. Stretching into the buggy she'd borrowed from her parents, she tucked one of the quilts she had brought with her around the nine-year-old girl who had already fallen back to sleep. Her niece would need some time to become accustomed to the early-to-bed and early-to-rise schedule of a farm. Last night, upon their arrival at the family's farm in Paradise Springs, the girl had been too wound up to sleep. This morning, Leah had caught sight of dampness on Mandy's cheeks before her niece hastily scrubbed her tears away.

For Leah, her homecoming was *wunderbaar. Mamm* had embraced her as if she never intended to let Leah go again. They had stayed up late to talk, pray and cry together. Her sole regret was her *daed* was away and wouldn't be back until next week. She hoped she could mend the hurt she and Johnny had caused him and that *Daed* would be as welcoming as her *mamm* had been.

It was never easy to tell with *Daed*. He kept many of his thoughts to himself, and he had never been as demonstrative as *Mamm*. Only Johnny, when he and *Daed* quarreled, had been able to break through that reserve.

No, she did not want to think of those loud arguments that had been the reason Johnny left and refused to return to Paradise Springs. She had done everything she could to try to persuade them both to listen to the other, but she had failed, and now it was too late.

Leah bent to pick up Shep and put him back in the buggy, but the little dog jumped out again, clearly thinking it was a game. Shep ran forward to the horse, who snorted a warning at him. The black dog was fascinated with the other animals on the farm, even the barn cats that had rewarded his curiosity with a scratch on the tip of his black nose.

"Stay, Shep," she said.

The little dog obeyed with an expression she was familiar with from Mandy. An expression that said, *All right, even though I don't want to.*

Sort of how she felt trying to make conversation with Ezra Stoltzfus. The last time she'd talked to him, words had flowed nonstop from both of them. Now it felt like they were strangers. With a start, she realized that was exactly what they were. She'd changed in many ways over the past ten years; surely he had, too.

If she needed proof, she got it when Ezra said in the same cool tone he used to greet her, "To be honest, Leah, I didn't expect to see you in Paradise Springs ever again."

"I wasn't sure I would ever get back here." She needed a safer subject, one where she didn't have to choose each word with care. "How are your sisters?"

"Ruth is married."

"She married before I left."

"True. She has seven *kinder* now."

"Did she choose names for them from Old Testament books as your parents did?"

His grin appeared and vanished so quickly she wondered if she'd truly seen it. "She decided to start with New Testament names."

"And how is Esther?"

"She is at home. *Mamm* moved into the *dawdi haus* after *Daed* died, and our baby sister is now giving orders to the Stoltzfus brothers to pick up after themselves and help with clearing the table after meals."

She hesitated. Asking about his siblings was not uncomfortable, but asking him how he was and what he was doing seemed too personal. That was silly. It wasn't as if she was going to quiz him about whether he was courting anyone. She'd never ask that. It wasn't their way to discuss possible matches before the young couple had their plans to marry announced during a church Sunday service. Even if such matters were discussed freely, she wouldn't ask Ezra such a private question. Not now when every nerve seemed on edge.

"What about you, Ezra?" she asked, keeping her voice light. "I don't see another shop here. What keeps you busy?"

"I took over the farm."

"As you planned to. Have you started your cheese-making business yet?"

His gaze darted away. Had she said too much? Or was he simply unsettled by each reminder of how differently her life had turned out from what she'd talked about while his had followed exactly the path he wanted?

He bent to pat the head of the little dog, who had inched over to smell his boots, but Shep shied away.

"Shep is skittish around people he doesn't know," she said. "He usually stayed inside except for his walks when we were in Philadelphia."

"Is that where you've been? Philadelphia? So close?"

She nodded, picking up the dog and holding him between her and Ezra like a furry shield. She was astonished by that thought. When they were growing up, she had never felt she needed to protect herself from Ezra. They'd been open about everything they felt and thought.

"Philadelphia is only fifty or sixty miles from here, and buses run from there to here regularly. Why haven't you come back to Paradise Springs?" he asked, and she noticed how much deeper his voice was than when they'd last spoken. Or maybe she'd forgotten its rich baritone. "Why didn't you come back for a visit?"

She gave him the answer she had perfected through the years, the answer that was partly the truth but left out much of what she felt in her heart. "I wanted to wait for my brother to come back with me."

"Did he?" Ezra glanced around the parking lot. "Is he here?"

Tears welled in her eyes, even though she'd been sure she had cried herself dry in recent days. "No. Johnny died two weeks ago." She regretted blurting out the news about her brother. How could Ezra have guessed when she wasn't wearing black? She was unsure how to explain that she had only a single plain dress until she and *Mamm* finished sewing a black one for her.

Ezra's face turned gray beneath his tan, and she recalled how Johnny and Ezra had been inseparable as small boys. That changed when they were around twelve or thirteen years old. Neither of them ever explained why, though she had pestered both of them to tell her.

"What happened?" he asked.

She crooked a finger for him to come away from the buggy. Even though the accident had happened shortly after Mandy was born, she didn't want to upset the *kind* by having her listen to the story again. Mandy was already distressed and desperate to return to Philadelphia and the life and friends she had there, but Leah hadn't considered—even for a second—leaving her niece behind with Mandy's best friend's family, who offered to take her in and rear her along with their *kinder*.

Mandy and she needed each other, because they had both lost the person at the center of their lives. Now they needed to go on alone. Not completely alone because they had each other and her parents and her two older sisters and their spouses and their extended family of cousins, aunts and uncles in Paradise Springs. And God, who had listened to Leah's prayers for the strength to live a plain life in the *Englisch* world.

Leah paused out of earshot of the sleeping girl and faced Ezra. The sunlight turned his brown hair to the shade of spun caramel that made his brown eyes look even darker. How many times she had teased him about his long lashes she had secretly envied! Then his eyes had crinkled with laughter, but now when she looked into those once-familiar eyes, she saw nothing but questions.

"Johnny was hurt in a really bad construction accident, and he never fully recovered." She looked down at Shep, who was whining at the mention of his master's name. The poor dog had been in mourning since her twin brother's death, and she had no idea how to comfort him. "In fact, Shep was his service dog." She stroked the dog's silken head.

"Why didn't you come home after Johnny was hurt?"

"He said he didn't want to be a burden on the community." She thought of the horrendous medical bills that had piled up and how she had struggled to pay what the insurance didn't cover. Johnny's friends told her that they should sue the construction company, but she had no idea how to hire an attorney. Instead, she had focused on her quilts, taking them to shops to sell them on consignment or to nearby craft fairs.

"No one is a burden in a time of need." Ezra frowned. "Both of you know that because you lived here when Ben Lee Chupp got his arm caught in the baler, and the doctors had to sew it back on. Everyone in our district and in his wife's district helped raise money to pay for his expenses. We would have gladly done the same for Johnny."

"I know, but Johnny didn't feel the same." She bit her

lip to keep from adding she was sure the financial obligations were not the main reason behind her brother's refusal. He had told her once, when he was in a deep melancholy, that he had vowed never to return home until their *daed* apologized to him for what *Daed* had said the night Johnny decided to leave.

That had never happened, and she had known it wouldn't. Johnny had inherited his stubbornness from *Daed*.

Ezra looked past her, and she turned to see Mandy standing behind her. Her niece was the image of Johnny, right down to the sprinkling of freckles across her apple-round cheeks. There might be something of Mandy's *mamm* in her looks, but Leah didn't remember much about the young *Englisch* woman who had never exchanged marriage vows with Johnny.

Leah knew her *mamm* had been pleased to see her granddaughter dressed in plain clothes at breakfast, and the dark green dress and white *kapp* did suit Mandy. However, Leah sensed Mandy viewed the clothing as dressing up, in the same way she had enjoyed wearing costumes and pretending to be a princess when she went to her best friend Isabella's house. Mandy seemed outwardly accepting of the abrupt changes in her life, but Leah couldn't forget the trails of tears on her niece's cheeks that morning.

Motioning for Mandy to come forward, she said with a smile, "This is Amanda, Johnny's daughter. We call her Mandy, and she is my favorite nine-year-old niece."

"I am your only nine-year-old niece, Aunt Leah." Mandy rolled her eyes with the eloquence of a preteen.

"*Ja*, you are, but you're my favorite one." She put her arm around Mandy's shoulders and gave them a squeeze.

"This is Ezra Stoltzfus. He lives on the farm on the other side of our fields."

"I spoke with your *daed* the day before yesterday," Ezra said as he looked from Mandy to Leah, "and he didn't say anything about you coming to visit."

"Coming home," Leah corrected in little more than a whisper.

"I see. Then I guess I should say welcome home, Leah." He didn't add anything else as he strode away.

She stood where she was and watched him go into his brother's buggy shop. When he did not look back, she sighed. She might have come home, but her journey back to the life she once had taken for granted had only begun.

Chapter Two

Ezra walked between the two rows of cows on the lower level of the white barn. He checked the ones being milked. The sound of the diesel generator from the small lean-to beyond the main barn rumbled through the concrete floor beneath his feet. It ran the refrigeration unit on the bulk tank where the milk was kept until it could be picked up by a trucker from the local processing plant.

He drew in a deep breath of the comforting scents of hay and grain and the cows. For most of his life, the place he'd felt most at ease was the bank barn. The upper floor was on the same level as the house and served as a haymow and a place to store the field equipment. On the lower level that opened out into the fields were the milking parlor and more storage.

He enjoyed working with the animals and watching calves grow to heifers before having calves of their own. He kept the best milkers and sold the rest so he could buy more Brown Swiss cows to replace the black-and-white Holsteins his *daed* had preferred. The gray-brown Swiss breed was particularly docile and well-known for producing milk with the perfect amount of cream for making cheese.

He hoped, by late summer, to be able to set aside enough milk to begin making cheese to sell. That was when the milk was at its sweetest and creamiest. He might have some soft cheese ready to be served during the wedding season in November or December if one of his bachelor brothers decided to get married.

He squatted and removed the suction milking can from a cow. He patted her back before carrying the heavy can to the bulk tank. She never paused in eating from the serving of grain he'd measured out for her. Opening the can, he emptied the milk into the tank. He closed both up and hooked the milking can to the next cow after cleaning her udder, a process he repeated thirty-one times twice a day.

Usually he used the time to pray and to map out what tasks he needed to do either that day or the next. Tonight, his thoughts were in a commotion, flitting about like a flock of frightened birds flying up from a meadow. He had not been able to rein them in since his remarkable conversation with Leah.

Johnny was dead. He found that unbelievable. Leah had come back and brought Johnny's *kind* with her. Even more unbelievable, though he had hoped for many years she would return to Paradise Springs.

Her *mamm* must be thrilled to have her and her niece home and devastated by Johnny's death. How would Abram react? The old man had not spoken his twins' names after they left. But Abram kept a lot to himself, and Ezra always wondered if Abram missed Leah and Johnny as much as the rest of his family did.

If his neighbor did not welcome his daughter and

granddaughter home, would Leah leave again and, this time, never come back?

"Think of something else," he muttered to himself as he continued the familiarly comforting process of milking.

"If you're talking to the cows, you're not going to get an answer," came his brother Isaiah's voice.

Ezra stood. Isaiah was less than a year younger than he was, and they were the closest among the seven Stoltzfus brothers. Isaiah had married Rose Mast the last week of December. He had been trying to grow his pale blond beard since then, but it remained patchy and uneven.

"If I got an answer," he said, leaning his arms on the cow's broad back, "I would need my head examined."

"That might not be a bad idea under the circumstances."

"Circumstances?"

Isaiah chuckled tersely. "Don't play dumb with me. I know Leah Beiler's reappearance in Paradise Springs must be throwing you for a loop. You two were really cozy before she left."

"We were friends. We'd been friends for years." *Friends who shared one perfect kiss one perfect night.* He wasn't about to mention that to his brother.

Isaiah was already worried about him. Ezra could tell from the dullness in his brother's eyes. Most of the time, they had a brightness that flickered in them like the freshly stirred coals in his smithy.

"Watch yourself," Isaiah said, as always the most cautious one in their family. "She jumped the fence once with her brother. Who knows? She may decide to do so again."

"I realize that."

"Gut."

"Gut," Ezra agreed, even though it was the last word he would have used to describe the situation.

His brother was right. When a young person left— jumped the fence, as it was called—they might return... for a while. Few were baptized into their faith, and most of them eventually drifted away again after realizing they no longer felt as if they belonged with their family and onetime friends.

While he finished the milking with Isaiah's help, they talked about when the crops should go in, early enough to get a second harvest but not so early the plants would be killed in a late frost. They talked about a new commission Isaiah had gotten at his smithy from an *Englisch* designer for a circular staircase. They talked about who might be chosen to become their next minister.

They talked about everything except the Beiler twins.

Ezra thanked his brother for his help as they turned the herd into the field as they always did after milking once spring arrived. Letting the cows graze in the pasture until nights got cold again instead of feeding them in the barn saved time and hay. When he followed Isaiah out of the barn and bade his brother a *gut* night, low clouds warned it would rain soon. The rest of his brothers were getting cleaned up at the outdoor pump before heading in for supper. Again, as they chatted about their day, everyone was careful *not* to talk about the Beilers, though he saw their curious looks in his direction.

As he washed his hands in the cold water, he couldn't keep himself from glancing across the fields to where the Beilers' house glowed with soft light in the thickening twilight. He jerked his gaze away. He should duck his head under the icy water and try to wash thoughts of Leah out of his brain.

Hadn't he learned anything in the past ten years? Did he want to endure that grief and uncertainty again? No! Well, there was his answer. He needed to stop thinking about her.

The kitchen was busy as it was every night, but even more so tonight because Joshua and his three *kinder* were joining them for supper. Most nights they did. Sometimes, Joshua cooked at his house down the road, or his young daughter attempted to prepare a meal.

With the ease of a lifetime of habit, the family gathered at the table. Joshua, as the oldest son, sat where *Daed* once did while *Mamm* sat at the foot of the table, close to the stove. The rest of them chose the seats they'd used their whole lives, and Joshua's younger son, Levi, claimed the chair across from Ezra, the chair where Isaiah had sat before he got married. Esther put two more baskets of rolls on the table, then took her seat next to *Mamm*. When Joshua bowed his head for silent prayer, the rest of them did as well.

Ezra knew he should be thanking God for the food in front of him, but all he could think of was his conversation with Leah and how he was going to have to get used to having her living across the fields again. He added a few hasty words of gratitude to his wandering prayer when Joshua cleared his throat to let them know grace was completed.

Bowls of potatoes and vegetables were passed around along with the platters of chicken and the baskets of rolls. Lost in his thoughts, Ezra didn't pay much attention to anything until he heard Joshua say, "Johnny Beiler is dead."

"Oh," *Mamm* said with a sigh, "I prayed that poor boy would come to his senses and return to Paradise Springs. What about Leah?"

Amos lowered his fork to his plate. "She came into the market today and asked if I would be willing to display some of her quilts for sale."

"What did you say?" asked Ezra, then wished he hadn't when his whole family looked at him.

"I said *ja*, of course." Amos frowned. "You know I always make room for any of our neighbors to sell their crafts. From what she said, she hopes to provide for her niece by selling quilts as she did when she was in Philadelphia."

Joshua looked up. "I have room for a few at the buggy shop. You know how many *Englisch* tourists we get wandering in to see the shop, and they love quilts."

"I will let her know." Amos smiled. "I'm sure she'll appreciate it."

"That is *gut* of you boys." Then *Mamm* asked, as she glanced around the table, "How is Leah doing?"

As if on cue, a knock sounded on the kitchen door. When Deborah, Joshua's youngest, ran to answer it, Ezra almost choked on his mouthful of chicken.

Leah and her niece stood there. For a moment, he was thrown back in time to the many occasions when Leah had come to the house to ask him to go berry picking or fishing or for a walk with her. As often, he'd gone to her house with an invitation to do something fun or a job they liked doing together.

But those days, he reminded himself sternly, were gone. And if he had half an ounce of sense, he'd make sure they never came back.

"I'm sorry to disturb your supper," Leah said, keeping her arm around Mandy as she stepped inside the warm kitchen where the Stoltzfus family gathered around the long trestle table. The room was almost identical to the one at her parents' house, except the walls behind the large woodstove that claimed one wall along with the newer propane stove were pale blue instead of green. Aware of the Stoltzfus eyes focused on them, she hurried to say, "Shep is missing, and we thought he might have come over here."

"Shep?" asked Esther. "Who is Shep?"

Leah smiled at Esther, who had been starting fourth grade when she and Johnny went away. Now she was a lovely young woman who must be turning the heads of teenage boys. When Esther returned her smile tentatively, Leah described the little black Cairn Terrier, which was unlike the large dogs found on farms in the area. Those dogs were working dogs, watching the animals and keeping predators away. Shep had had his own tasks, and Leah wondered what the poor pup thought now that he didn't need to perform them. Did he feel as lost as she did?

"Let me get a flashlight, and I'll help you search." Ezra pushed back his chair and got up.

His brothers volunteered to help, too, but everyone froze when Mandy said, "I didn't know Amish could use flashlights. I thought you didn't use electricity."

Heat rose up Leah's cheeks, and she guessed they were crimson. "Mandy..."

"Let the *kind* ask questions, Leah," Wanda, Ezra's *mamm,* said with a gentle smile. "How else do we learn if we don't ask questions? I remember you had plenty of questions of your own when you were her age." She patted the bench beside her. "Why don't you sit here with Deborah and me? You can have the last piece of snitz pie while we talk."

"Snitz?" asked Mandy with an uneasy glance at Leah. "What's a snitz?"

"Dried apple pie." Leah smiled. "Wanda makes a delicious snitz pie."

"Better than Grandma's?"

Wanda patted Mandy's hand and brought the *kind* to sit beside her. "Your *grossmammi* is a *wunderbaar* cook. There is no reason to choose which pie is better when God has given you the chance to enjoy both." Behind the girl's back, she motioned for Leah and her sons to begin their search for the missing dog.

While Ezra's brothers headed into the storm, Leah went out on the back porch and grimaced. It was raining. She should have paused to grab a coat before leaving the house, but Mandy was desolate at the idea of losing Shep. When Mandy asked if the dog had gone "home to Philly," Leah's heart had threatened to break again. The little girl didn't say much about her *daed*'s death, but Leah knew it was on her mind all the time.

As it was on her own.

"Here."

She smiled as Ezra held out an open umbrella to her. "Thank you."

He snapped another open at the same time he switched on a flashlight. "Where should we look?"

"Shep likes other animals. Let's look in your barn first, and then we can search the fields if we don't find him."

"I hope he hasn't taken it into his head to chase my cows."

She shook her head. "From the way he's reacted to cows and horses, I don't think he knows quite what they are. He is curious. Nothing more."

"Let's hope he's in the barn. There have been reports

of coydogs in the area. Some of our neighbors have lost chickens."

Leah shuddered. The feral dogs that were half coyote were the bane of a farmer's life. They were skilled hunters and not as afraid of humans as other wild animals were. Little Shep wouldn't stand a chance against the larger predator.

As they left the lights from the house behind, she added, "Thanks for helping. I didn't mean to make you leave in the middle of supper."

"Your niece looked pretty upset, and Esther offered to keep our suppers warm in the oven. The cows are this way."

"I remember."

He didn't answer as they walked to the milking parlor. Spraying the light into the lower floor, he remained silent as she called Shep's name.

"I missed this," she murmured.

"Walking around in the rain?"

She shook her head and tilted her umbrella to look up at him. "Barn scents. The city smelled of heat off the concrete and asphalt, as well as car exhaust and the reek of trash before it was picked up. I missed the simple odors of this life."

"You could have come home."

"Not without Johnny." Her voice broke as she added, "Even though when I finally came back, he didn't come with me."

"I'm sorry he is dead, Leah. I should have said so before." He paused as they closed their umbrellas and walked together between the gutters in the milking parlor. "My only excuse is that I was shocked to see you."

"I understand." She shouted the dog's name. The conversation was wandering into personal areas, and she wanted to avoid going in that direction.

She wouldn't have come over to the Stoltzfus family home tonight if *Mamm* hadn't mentioned possibly seeing Shep racing through the field between their farms. Even then, she would have suggested waiting until daylight to search for the pup except that Mandy was in tears.

"I don't think Shep is here," she said after a few minutes of spraying the corners with light.

"Let's walk along the fence. Maybe he's close enough to hear you and will come back." His grim face suggested he was unsure they would find Shep tonight.

She put up her umbrella so she didn't have to look at his pessimistic frown. If she did, she might not be able to halt herself from asking where the enthusiastic, happy young man she'd known had vanished to.

How foolish she had been to think nothing would change!

If she could turn back the clock, she might never have gone with Johnny that night when he promised her ice cream and then took her far from everything she'd ever known. She sighed silently. Johnny had asked her to come with him because he needed her. Not that he had any idea then how much he would come to depend on her, but she had always rescued him from other predicaments. Maybe he had hoped she would save him that time, too, but he was too deeply involved with Carleen, his pregnant *Englisch* girlfriend, by then.

Leah wondered what Ezra was thinking as they walked along the fence enclosing the pasture. She guessed she'd be smarter not to ask. He remained silent, so the only sound was the plop of raindrops on the umbrellas except when she shouted for the dog.

Because of that, she was able to hear a faint bark. It was coming from the direction of the creek that divided the Stoltzfus farm from her parents'. She ran through the wet grass, not paying attention to how her umbrella flopped behind her and rain pelted her face.

Ezra matched her steps, his flashlight aimed out in front of them. He put out an arm, and she slid to a stop before striking it.

"Careful," he said. "You don't want to fall in the creek tonight."

"The bank—"

"Collapsed two years ago, and the water is closer than you remember."

"Danki."

He nodded at her thanks but said nothing more.

How had the talkative boy become this curt man? What had happened to him in the years after she left Paradise Springs? She wanted to ask that as much as she wanted to find Shep, but she didn't.

Calling out the dog's name again, she relaxed when she heard a clatter in the brush. "Ezra, point the flashlight a little farther to the left."

"Here?"

She almost put her hand on his arm to guide him but pulled back. Even a casual touch would be foolish. "A bit farther."

She let out a cry of joy when light caught in two big eyes and Shep yipped a greeting. She squatted as he burst out of the brush. He leaped up and put his paws on her knees, the signal he had learned to show he was ready to assist. With a gasp, she stood and stared at the pair of paw prints on the front of her skirt.

Shep deflated as if he had been scolded.

Bending over, she patted his soaked head. "Come, Shep. Stay with us."

He jumped to his feet, his tail wagging wildly. His tongue lolled out of the side of his mouth in what was his doggy smile.

"Do you have a leash for him?" Ezra asked as she turned to walk back to the house with Shep happily trotting by her side far enough away so the rain didn't run off the umbrella onto him. "If he ran away once, he'll run again."

Was he talking about the dog, or was he speaking of her, too? He'd made it clear he didn't think she intended to stay in Paradise Springs. Pretending to take his words at face value, she said, "Shep is fine now that he has something he knows he should do." She smiled sadly while they crossed the field back toward the house. "I need to keep him busy. He's a service dog, not a pet."

"You called him a service dog before. What does that mean?" He glanced at the dog and jumped back when Shep shook himself.

"Shep!" cried Mandy as she and Deborah ran from the house. "You found him! You found him!"

Leah snagged Shep's collar before he could run up the porch stairs and get the two girls wet. She sent the girls to ask Wanda for some towels so they could dry off the dog and themselves. She didn't want to track mud into the house.

"Old ones," she called after them. As soon as the screen door slammed in their wake, she turned back to Ezra. "You asked what a service dog is. They are dogs trained to help people who need assistance with everyday things."

"I've seen *Englisch* tourists with guide dogs. Usually

German shepherds. What kind of service can something Shep's size do?"

"Don't let his size fool you. Shep is one-third heart, one-third brain, and one-third nose. After the accident, Johnny often had seizures. If he was doing something, like getting from his bed to his wheelchair, he could fall and be hurt. Shep helped by alerting us to an upcoming seizure."

"A dog can do that?" He stepped aside when Amos came out on the porch with ragged towels.

"Heard you had a very wet dog out here." He chuckled. "I can see the girls weren't exaggerating."

Taking a towel and thanking him, grateful for his acceptance of her as she'd been when he greeted her at his store as if she'd never left, Leah began drying the dog. She looked up at Ezra and said, "I didn't believe it myself at first. The doctor told us some dogs can sense a change in a person's odor that happens just before a seizure." She gave Shep another rub, leaving the dog's hair stuck up in every direction. "He let us know about Johnny's seizures. That way, we could be sure Johnny was secure so he wouldn't hit things when the seizures started. After we got Shep, Johnny no longer was covered with bruises."

Ezra picked up the damp dog and rubbed his head. Shep rewarded him with a lick on the cheek.

"He likes you!" Mandy rushed out onto the porch. "Look, Aunt Leah! Esther gave me some of her date cookies. They're yummy!" She paused, then reached into her apron pocket. "She sent some out for you, too."

Ezra put the dog down and took the crumbling cookie she held out to him. Shep lapped up the crumbs the second they hit the ground.

"Can Deborah come over and play?" Mandy leaned into Leah and said in a whisper, "She's my age, you know."

"I'm sure something can be arranged soon." Leah took a bite of her cookie and smiled. Esther clearly had learned her *mamm*'s skills in the kitchen. "But for now, let's get Shep back home so we can get him dried off before he catches a cold. *Guten owed*, Ezra."

"What did you say?" Mandy asked.

"Good evening. It's time for us to go home."

The girl yawned but shook her head. "I want another cookie."

"Not tonight."

"But I want another cookie." Mandy's lower lip struck out in the pout she had perfected with Johnny, who could never tell her no. Whether it was because he felt guilty that he was an invalid or he had never married her *mamm*, he had been determined to make it up to his daughter in every possible way. However, the girl should have learned by now that such antics were far less successful with Leah.

"We will come back and visit soon," Leah said quietly.

"When?"

Aware of Ezra listening, Leah said, "Soon. Let's go."

Mandy grumbled something under her breath, and Leah decided it would be wise not to ask her to repeat it.

Calling to Shep to come with them, Leah turned to the porch stairs. She bit back a gasp when Ezra moved between her and the steps. He frowned at her as if she were as young as Mandy.

"Wait here," he said in a voice that brooked no defiance.

But she retorted anyhow. "It's late, and Mandy needs to go home so she can get some sleep."

"You plan on walking in this downpour?"

She looked past him and saw it was raining even harder than before, though she would not have guessed that possible. Wind whipped it almost sideways. Even so, she said, "I'll share the umbrella with Mandy. We'll be fine."

"You cannot handle a dog, a *kind* and an umbrella by yourself in this wind. Let me get the buggy, and I'll drive you home."

"Don't be silly, Ezra. It is only across the field."

"You're not going across the field in the dark. You know that could be too dangerous. If you go by the road, it's a quarter mile down our farm lane and a half mile along a dark road, then another quarter mile for your farm lane. That's a mile with two squirming creatures." He took the umbrella out of her hand. "Wait here until I get the horse hitched up."

"Ezra—"

"Listen to *gut* sense, Leah. Just this once."

Pricked by his cool words, which she knew were true—as far as he knew—she fired back, "I was going to say *danki*."

He opened his mouth to say something, then seemed to think better of it. Repeating his order for her to wait on the porch, he strode toward the barn.

In his wake, Mandy asked, "Is he always this angry?"

"I don't know," she had to reply because she was realizing more each time she saw Ezra how little she knew the man he had become.

Chapter Three

The family buggy usually felt spacious with its double rows of seats, but, tonight, it seemed too small when Ezra stepped in and picked up the reins from the dash. He flipped the switch that turned on the lamps attached to the front and back of the buggy. They were run by a battery under the backseat where Leah's niece and his, who had begged to come along, were whispering and giggling as if they'd known each other all their lives.

No, not like that, because Leah and he *had* known each other all their lives, and silence had settled like a third passenger on the seat between them.

"Ready?" he asked as he turned on the wiper that kept his side of the windshield clear.

Instead of answering him directly, Leah called back, "Do you have Shep with you, girls?"

"He's here." Mandy burst into laughter again. "Oops! He stuck his nose under my dress. His whiskers tickle."

"It sounds as if we're set," Leah said, but she didn't look at him. Her hands were folded on her lap, and her elbows were pressed close to her sides.

Did she sense the invisible wall between them, too?

Ezra nodded and slapped the reins to get the horse moving. The rainy night seemed to close in around them while they drove down the straight farm lane. He flipped on the signal and looked both ways along the deserted country road. Not many people would be out on such a rainy night.

He racked his brain for something to say to break the smothering quiet in the front seat. Everything he could come up with seemed too silly or too personal. Listening to the girls talking easily in the back, he couldn't help remembering how he and Leah used to chat like that. About everything and nothing. About important things and things that didn't really matter.

"Leah—" he began.

"Ezra—" she said at the same time.

"Go ahead," they both said at once.

Mandy leaned forward and giggled. "How do you do that? Can you keep talking together?"

"I doubt it," he said at the same time Leah echoed him.

That sent the girls into peals of laughter.

"They are easily entertained," Ezra said, risking a glance toward Leah.

"I've noticed. I hope they will become *gut* friends. It will help for Mandy to have someone she knows when she starts school next week."

"You are sending her to school here?"

"Of course." She looked at him and said, "You don't believe we're here to stay, do you?"

"I don't know what to believe." He wasn't going to admit he was unsure if he was more bothered by the idea she might go away again or that she might stay. Either way, he needed to keep his feelings as under control and to himself as her *daed* did his. *Ja*, he needed to act as Abram would.

"Believe *me*," she retorted. "You always did."

"Before."

She recoiled as if he had struck her. He wished he'd thought before he'd spoken. He didn't want his frustration to lash out at her.

"Leah," he began again, but was interrupted by the honk of a car horn.

He stiffened when he looked back and saw a car racing toward them. The driver leaned on the horn. He pulled the buggy toward the right, feeling the wheels jerk in the mud.

The girls cried out in alarm as the car cut close to them, sending water rising over the top of the carriage. He fought to keep the buggy from tipping as he twisted it farther off the road.

Gripping the reins in one hand, he wrapped his other arm around Leah as she slid into him. His breath erupted out of him when his shoulder struck the buggy's side. Pain ricocheted down his arm and numbed his fingers, but he kept hold of both the reins and Leah.

The car careened past them. He steered the horse onto the road at an angle that wouldn't send the buggy onto its side. The wheels burst out of the mud and spun on the wet road. He slowed the horse as the car's taillights vanished over a hill and into the darkness. Warm breath brushed his neck, and he was abruptly aware of Leah sitting within the curve of his arm. She clutched one of his suspenders, and he could see her lips moving in what he was sure was a prayer.

She raised her face, and his breath caught as he realized how long it had been since the other time he had held her close. That night he had surrendered to his longing to kiss her. Tonight…

As if she could read his thoughts, Leah pushed herself away and moved to the far side of the seat. Her fingers quivered as she smoothed her *kapp* into place.

"Is everyone okay?" she asked, and her voice trembled, as well.

He doubted the girls noticed as they both began to talk about the car that had rushed past them. Shep's yip announced the dog was all right, too.

As Deborah and Mandy began analyzing every aspect of the near accident, Ezra guided the buggy along the road. He kept an eye out for any other cars and noticed Leah doing the same, though most drivers were cautious around buggies and bicycles and pedestrians.

"I don't think the driver even saw us," she said, surprising him that she didn't let them lapse into silence again. "Not until the car was right behind us."

"He should have noticed the lights and the slow-moving vehicle sign on the back. When headlights hit it, the colors flare up as bright as a candle."

"That was rude," Mandy interjected. "Splashing us." She looked down at the floor where water was gathering into puddles. "Shep is getting wet again."

"We'll dry him off when we get home," Leah replied.

Ezra turned the buggy into the farm lane leading to the Beilers' house, and he heard Leah's sigh of relief. Even the girls in the back became silent as he drove toward the farmhouse set behind the barns.

It was almost the twin of his home, except there never were any lights on in the *dawdi haus*, which had been empty for as long as he could remember. He slowed the buggy and drew as close to the porch steps as he could, so Leah and her niece wouldn't get too wet.

She climbed out and took Shep before Mandy bounced up onto the porch. With a wave, the girl rushed into the house with the dog following close behind.

Leah started to follow, then said, "*Danki* for the ride home, Ezra." She shuddered so hard he could see it ripple along her. "When I think of that driver speeding past us while Mandy and I might have been walking along the road, it's terrifying."

"Don't think about it."

"But I must because I need to thank God for keeping us safe tonight when we could have been hurt." She clasped her hands together so tightly her knuckles grew pale. "When I think of something happening to Mandy, I can't stand it."

"God was watching over us tonight."

"I pray He watches over the driver in that car, too, so he or she gets home safely without endangering anyone else."

"You still think of others before yourself, don't you?"

"You make that sound as if it's wrong."

"It can be."

Her eyes widened, and she followed her niece into the house without another word.

"Why is Leah upset?" asked Deborah from the back.

He had forgotten his niece was a witness to the brief conversation. Maybe it was for the best they hadn't said more.

So why did it feel as if there were many things he should have said?

Within a few days, Leah could easily have felt as if she had never left home, but no one else seemed willing to let her forget it. Each person coming to the house began with questions about her time in Philadelphia and ended with how happy they were she had returned. She appreciated their *gut* wishes, but she was tired of relating the same story over and over and seeing no understanding in their eyes. Maybe it was something only a twin could comprehend. When one twin was in trouble, the other twin could not rest easily until she helped him out of trouble. That was the way it had always been for her and Johnny.

Her heart sang with joy when her sister Martha arrived for a visit with her five *kinder*. Her other sister had moved to Indiana with her husband within a year after Leah left, but Martha lived near the southern edge of Paradise Springs.

The two older *kinder* were a few years younger than Mandy, and they soon were outside teaching her how to gather eggs and feed the chickens. Their lighthearted voices followed the soft breeze through the open kitchen window.

Leah sat in a rocking chair by the table and bounced the youngest on her knee. She carefully removed her *kapp* strings from his eager fingers. Beside her sister, who sat where she always had at the table, two other small *kinder* watched Leah warily. The little boy stuck his thumb in his mouth while the girl had two fingers in hers. Leah remembered Mandy doing the same as a toddler. Joyous shouts from the yard announced her niece was having fun with her new cousins.

"Five *kinder* and another on the way." Leah smiled. "I am going to have fun getting to know them."

"I'm glad they will have a chance to know you." Martha glanced down at them. "They are shy."

Reaching out to her sister, Leah put her hand on Martha's. She had missed her family dreadfully while away, and she was thankful for this chance to reconnect with them. "We have plenty of time to get to know one another."

"It is lovely for my *kinder* to have another cousin." Tears rolled up into Martha's eyes. "And for us to have something of Johnny in our family. To think we had no idea she even existed…" She shook her head and looked away as her tears glistened at the corner of her eyes.

"I wrote home often, though I know you didn't see any of my letters." She wondered if she should have said that. She didn't want to ruin the warmth of this moment with her sister and *Mamm*.

"Why not?" asked Martha, her eyes wide.

Mamm said quietly, "Your *daed* sent back the letters unread, Martha. He felt, Leah, that, if you truly wanted to ease our worries about you and Johnny, you'd come back to Paradise Springs and tell us yourself."

"But Johnny wasn't able to travel." Leah sighed, wishing her *daed* and her brother hadn't been so stubborn.

Mamm's eyes shone with the tears that appeared whenever Johnny's accident was mentioned. Even though it had happened over nine years ago, *Mamm* hadn't learned about it until Leah returned home.

"I know that now," *Mamm* said.

"Will *Daed* understand?" She couldn't keep anxiety from her voice.

"You need to ask him yourself."

"I will when he gets home."

Martha and *Mamm* exchanged a glance she wasn't able to decipher before Martha said, "He will forgive you, Leah. That is our way, but you can't expect him to forget how you and Johnny left without even telling us where you were going. Just sneaking away."

Leah opened her mouth to protest she hadn't intended to leave, but saying that wouldn't change anything. She *had* gone with Johnny, and she had chosen not to come back while he needed her. Shutting her mouth, she wondered if her family felt as Ezra did, and they were waiting for her to disappear again. How could she convince them otherwise? She had no idea.

Ezra stopped in midstep when he came out of the upper level of the barn. What was a kid doing standing on the lower rail of the fence around the cow pasture and hanging over it? He should know better than to stand there. Surely even an *Englisch* boy knew better.

He realized it wasn't a boy. It was a girl, dressed in jeans and a bright green T-shirt. Leah's niece, Mandy. She wore *Englisch* clothing, unlike what she'd had on when he saw her before. Her hair, the exact same shade of gold as Leah's, was plaited in an uneven braid, and he suspected she'd done it herself. Her sneakered feet balanced on the lower rail on the fence, and she was stretching out her hand to pet the nose of his prized pregnant Brown Swiss cow.

"Don't do that!" he called as he leaned his hoe against the barn door.

She jumped down and whirled to face him, staring at him with those eyes so like Leah's. "I wasn't doing anything." She clasped her hands behind her back as if she feared something on them would contradict her.

He went to where she stood. When she didn't turn and run away as some kids would have, he was reminded again of her aunt. Leah never had backed down when she believed she was right.

The thought took the annoyed edge off his voice. "You shouldn't bother her."

"Ezra is right," said Leah as she walked toward them with the grace of a cloud skimming the sky.

He couldn't look away. So many times he had imagined seeing her walk up the lane again, but he'd doubted it ever would happen. Now it had, and it seemed as unreal as those dreams.

"She needs peace and quiet," Leah went on, "because she's going to have a calf soon."

"Calf?" The little girl's face crinkled in puzzlement. "I thought they were called fawns."

"No." She tried not to smile. "Deer have fawns. Cows have calves."

"But that's not a cow."

"She definitely is," he said, resting his elbow on the topmost rail.

Mandy put her hands at the waist of her jeans and gave them both a look that suggested they were trying to tease her and she'd have none of it. "*That* isn't a cow. Everyone knows cows are black and white. That is light brown. Like a deer."

Now it was his turn to struggle not to smile. "Some cows are black and white." He pointed to the ones grazing in the Beilers' field. "But others are brown or plain black or even red."

"Red?"

"More of a reddish-brown," Leah said.

"Then why are all the cows in my books black and white?" Mandy asked, not ready to relent completely.

Leah shrugged, her smile finally appearing. "Maybe

those *Englisch* artists had seen only black-and-white cows."

Ezra didn't hear what else she said, because his gaze focused on the dimple on her left cheek. How he used to tease her about it! Had she known he was halfway serious even then when he said God had put it in her cheek to keep her face from being perfect? He hadn't been much older than Mandy the first time he said that.

"Does she have a name?" Mandy asked.

He replied, "I call her Bessie."

She wrinkled her nose. "Everyone calls their cows Bessie." She glanced at her aunt, then added, "At least in books. She's pretty and nice. She should have a special name of her own."

"What would you suggest?" he asked, wanting to prolong the conversation but knowing he was being foolish.

He saw his surprise reflected on Leah's face when Mandy said, "I think you should call her *Mamm Millich*. That's *Deitsch*, you know, for Mommy Milk. Grandma Beiler has been teaching me some words." She giggled. "They feel funny on my tongue when I say them."

"I think it's a *wunderbaar* name," he said. "*Mamm Millich* she is."

"I named a cow!" Mandy bounced from one foot to the other in her excitement. "I can't wait to tell Isabella! She'll never believe this." She faltered. "But there's no phone. How can I tell her?"

"Why don't you write her a letter about *Mamm Millich*?" Leah asked. "Think how excited she'll be."

"But I won't be able to hear her being excited. I miss Isabella. I want to *tell* her about *Mamm Millich*."

He watched as Leah bent so her eyes were level with her niece's. Compassion filled her voice as she said, "I know, Mandy, but we must abide by the *Ordnung*'s rules here in Paradise Springs."

"They're stupid rules!" She spun on her heel and ran several steps before turning and shouting, "Stupid rules! I hate them, and I hate being here. I want to go home! To Philadelphia! Why didn't you let me stay with Isabella? *She* loves me and wants me to be happy. If you really loved me like you say you do, you wouldn't have made me come to this weird place with these weird rules."

"Mandy, you know I love you. I…" Leah's voice faded into a soft sob as her niece sped away.

When Leah's shoulders sagged as if she carried a burden too heavy for her to bear any longer, Ezra's first thought was to find a way to ease it. But what could he do? It was Leah's choice—hers and her family's—what Mandy's future would be. He was only a neighbor.

"I'm sorry you had to hear that," Leah said as she stared at the now empty lane. "The change has been harder on her than I expected it to be. I tried to live plain in the city, but Johnny consented to letting her have a cell phone, which he allowed her to use whenever she wanted."

"So he didn't want her to grow up with our ways?"

"It wasn't that. It was more he couldn't deny her anything she wanted."

Seeing the grief in her eyes, he wondered if she was thinking of her brother or her niece or both of them. "Why isn't Mandy with her *mamm*?"

"I don't know where she is. After Johnny's accident, Carleen spent more and more time away from the apartment. One day she was gone. She left a note saying that she couldn't handle the situation any longer. She refused to marry Johnny because she wasn't ready to settle down.

She surely hadn't expected to be tied down to an invalid." Her voice grew taut. "Or tied down to a baby. She took the money we had, as well as everything that was hers, and vanished. We never heard from her again."

"Does Mandy know?"

She shook her head. "Johnny and I shielded her from the truth. No *kind* should think she's unwanted." Squaring her shoulders, she said, "But Mandy isn't unwanted. In spite of what she said, she knows I love her, and she's already beginning to love her family here. She will adjust soon."

"And what about you?"

She frowned at him. "What do you mean? I'm happy to be back home, and I don't have much to adjust to other than the quiet at night. Philadelphia was noisy."

"I wasn't talking about that." He hesitated, not sure how to say what he wanted without hurting her feelings.

"Oh." Her smile returned, but it was unsteady. "You're talking about us. We aren't *kinder* any longer, Ezra. I'm sure we can be reasonable about this strange situation we find ourselves in," she said in a tone that suggested she wasn't as certain as she sounded. Uncertain of him or of herself?

"I agree."

"We are neighbors again. We're going to see each other regularly, but it'd be better if we keep any encounters to a minimum." She faltered before hurrying on. "Who knows? We may even call each other friend again someday, but until then, it'd probably be for the best if you live your life and I live mine." She backed away. "Speaking of that, I need to go and console Mandy." Taking one step, she halted. "*Danki* for letting her name the cow. That made her happier than I've seen her since…"

She didn't finish. She didn't have to. His heart cramped as he thought of the sorrow haunting both Leah and Mandy. They had both lost someone very dear to them, the person Leah had once described to him as "the other half of myself."

The very least he could do was agree to her request that was to everyone's benefit. Even though he knew she was right, he also knew there was no way he could ignore Leah Beiler.

Yet, somehow, he needed to figure out how to do exactly that.

Chapter Four

As soon as she opened her eyes as the sun was rising, Leah heard the soft lilt of her *mamm*'s singing while she prepared the cold breakfast they ate each Sunday. It was the sound she had awakened to almost every day of her life until she went away with Johnny. It was only on rare occasions when *Mamm* was helping a neighbor or the few times she'd been too sick to get out of bed that her voice wasn't the first thing Leah heard each morning.

Leah slid out from beneath the covers, taking care not to jostle Mandy. A nightmare had brought her running from the room across the hall. As one had every night since they arrived on the farm a week ago.

Maybe she should ask Mandy to share her room. She could bring in the small cot that was kept for when they had more guests than beds. It wasn't the most comfortable cot, but she would let Mandy use the double bed where Leah had slept during her childhood. Leah suspected she'd get a better night's sleep on the cot than being roused in the middle of the night by a frightened little girl who kicked and squirmed while she slept. Had

Mandy always been restless, or was she bothered by her dreams even after she crawled into bed with Leah?

Going to the window where faint sunlight edged around the dark green shade, Leah looked out. The rain she'd heard during the night had left the grass sparkling at dawn as if stars had been strewn across the yard. She smiled when she noticed the barn door was open and the cows in the field.

Her hand clutched the molding around the window when she saw *Daed* emerge from the chicken coop. Like Johnny, he was not too tall, but very spare. The early light sparkled off silver in his hair and beard, silver that hadn't been there years ago. When had he arrived home? It must have been very late, because she hadn't heard a vehicle come up the farm lane.

She started to pray for the right words to speak when she came face-to-face with her *daed* for the first time in a decade. Her silent entreaty faltered when, instead of striding toward the house at his usual swift pace that made short work of any distance, he put one hand on the low roof while he placed the other on his brow. He stood like that for a long moment before looking at the house. His shoulders rose and fell in a sigh before he pushed himself away from the coop. With every step toward the house, his steps grew steadier and closer to the length of his normal stride.

Was her *daed* sick? Perhaps he had picked up some sort of bug at the auction. Or was it more serious?

Leah hurried to get dressed, making sure no speck of lint was visible on her black dress or cape. Settling her *kapp* on her hair that was pulled back in its proper bun, she stared at herself in the mirror over the dresser. She was not the girl who had left Paradise Springs, but she suddenly felt as young and unprepared for what awaited her as she had been that night.

Trying not to act like a naughty *kind* sneaking through the house, she went down the back stairs. She opened the door at the bottom and stepped into the kitchen.

Mamm wore her Sunday best and aimed a smile at Leah as she set the oatmeal muffins she had baked last night in the center of the kitchen table. At one end, *Daed* sat in his chair. There was a hint of grayness beneath his deep tan from years of working in the fields, and she could not help noticing how the fingers on his right hand trembled on the edge of the table.

Was he ill, or was he as nervous as she was?

She got her answer when he said in his no-nonsense voice, "Sit, Leah. We don't want to be late for Sunday service."

She obeyed, keeping her head down so neither he nor her *mamm* could see the tears burning her eyes.

"Is Mandy asleep?" asked *Mamm* gently as she took her chair at the foot of the table.

"Ja," Leah answered. "She didn't sleep well last night." She glanced at her *daed*, who had remained silent save for his terse order.

What had she expected? For him to welcome her home as the *daed* had in the parable of the prodigal son? *Daed* wasn't demonstrative. While *Mamm* spoke of how she loved her family, *Daed* had never uttered those words to his *kinder*. Yet, he had shown her in many ways that she was important. Her favorite had been when he asked her to ride into Paradise Springs with him so they could have special time together.

Be patient, she told herself. The words from James's

epistle filled her mind. *But let patience have her perfect work, that ye may be perfect and entire, wanting nothing.*

As if she had repeated those words aloud, *Daed* bowed his head to signal the beginning of grace. Leah did the same. During the silent prayer, she asked God not only for patience but for Him to open *Daed's* heart and let her back in. God's help might be the only way that would happen.

When her *daed* cleared his throat to let them know grace was over, she looked at him again. He poured a hearty serving of corn flakes into his bowl, then handed the open box to her.

"*Danki,*" she murmured.

He did not reply but set several of the muffins on his plate. Again he passed the food to her.

"*Danki,*" she said more loudly.

Again he acted as if she had not spoken.

She bit her lower lip and handed the plate to her *mamm* without taking a single muffin. Her appetite was gone. Her *daed* clearly intended to act as if she were nothing but an unwelcome outsider who had invaded their family. It was almost like he had put her under the *Meidung.* She wasn't actually being shunned, of course, because he was willing to sit at the table with her and he handed her the plates. However, he did not speak to her or look in her direction unless absolutely necessary. Silence settled around the table, and she had no idea how to break it.

She almost cheered with relief when footsteps pounded down the stairs. *Mamm* rose quickly when the door at the base opened and Mandy emerged, yawning and rubbing her eyes. She had dressed, but her hair hung down her back in a disheveled braid that she'd worn to bed.

"I need help with my hair," Mandy announced.

"Ja." Leah started to stand.

Mamm motioned for her to stay where she was. Taking Mandy by the hand, *Mamm* led her to the table and toward the end where *Daed* sat.

Mandy shot an uneasy glance at Leah. Even though she wished she could reassure her niece that everything was fine, Leah said nothing as she waited to see how her *daed* would act when meeting the granddaughter he hadn't known he had. Again she noticed how his hand was shaking until he put his left one on top of it as he leaned forward.

"This is *Grossdawdi* Abram, Mandy," *Mamm* said with a smile. "He has been eager to meet you."

Mandy regarded him with hesitation, and Leah wondered if she was disconcerted by *Daed*'s long, thick beard. She had seen the little girl staring at other men who wore beards, especially those that reached to the middle of their chests. Even though Leah had explained many times during their years in Philadelphia about how the Amish dressed and why, Mandy seemed uneasy around the married men with their full beards.

Leah had tried to hide her own unsettled reaction when Mandy asked why Ezra was clean shaven. She had seemed startled that he wasn't married. Leah had to admit that she was, too. His older brother and sister had wed years ago, and Isaiah, who was less than a year younger than Ezra, married last year. It probably wouldn't be long before the others found spouses, including the youngest Stoltzfus, Esther. With his *mamm* already depending on Esther's help, she couldn't handle the household chores by herself. Ezra needed a wife, so why hadn't he found one by now?

Telling herself that was a question best left unexplored,

she watched as *Mamm* bent to whisper in Mandy's ear. The little girl leaned forward and gave *Daed* a tentative kiss on the cheek. Leah held her breath, not sure how her *daed* would react.

She swallowed her shocked gasp when *Daed* lightly stroked Mandy's cheek as he said, "You are as pretty as your *grossmammi* was when she was your age, ain't so?"

That was all the encouragement Mandy needed to begin chatting as if she wanted to catch up her *grossdawdi* on everything that had happened from the day she was born. She barely slowed down to eat and paid no attention when Leah reminded her that it was rude to speak with her mouth full of food. She asked about the animals on the farm and told him about Shep.

Only because she was watching did Leah notice *Daed* wince when Mandy began talking about how Shep had helped alert them to Johnny's seizures. When he abruptly said it was time for another prayer before they left the table, he gave them no time to bow their heads before he'd pushed back his chair and was striding to the back door. He called back over his shoulder that the buggy would be ready to leave in a few minutes.

Mandy looked at Leah. "Did I say something wrong?"

"Of course not. We simply don't want to be late for the worship service," *Mamm* answered before Leah could. Coming to her feet, she picked up the almost empty muffin plate. "Leah, help Mandy with her hair while I clear the table."

Leah brushed out her niece's hair, braided it and wound it around her head properly with the ease of years of practice. Sending Mandy back upstairs to get her white, heart-shaped *kapp* and her black bonnet, she began picking up the dirty dishes and stacking them by the sink where they could be washed once the Sabbath was past.

"That went well," she said without looking at her *mamm*. "*Daed* seemed very glad to see Mandy."

"Why shouldn't he be? Mandy is a sweet, *gut kind*. You've brought her up well."

Warmth spread through the iciness that had clamped around Leah from the moment she witnessed her *daed*'s weakness by the chicken coop. She considered asking her *mamm* if *Daed* was feeling poorly but had to wonder if she'd misconstrued what she saw. After a long trip away, *Daed* probably was exhausted. Could that explain his terse reaction to her homecoming? She longed to believe that was so.

"*Danki*. I made sure that we lived a *gut* Christian life while we were away," Leah replied.

"I know you well, daughter. I have never doubted that you did your best to live as you were taught. Since you brought Mandy home, I have seen how you made efforts to teach her our ways and our beliefs."

"If you see that, why can't *Daed*?" She clapped her hand over her mouth, but it was too late. She'd blurted out the words from the depths of her aching heart.

"I warned you. He was hurt and humiliated when you left. To lose two *kinder* when they jumped the fence…" *Mamm* shook her head and sighed.

"But I didn't jump the fence."

"You left." She turned to the stairs as Mandy bounced down into the kitchen.

Leah didn't answer as her *mamm* checked that Mandy's bonnet was properly tied beneath her chin before her niece rushed out to watch *Daed* harness the horse to the buggy. Leah wasn't sure what she could have said. She *had* left…

to go with Johnny and persuade him to return, though she never had succeeded with that. Was her failure why *Daed* was so upset with her? That she'd never convinced his only son to come home?

Again those traitorous tears welled up in her eyes. She longed to ask her *daed* why he hadn't read even one of her letters. It had been difficult to steal time away from taking care of an invalid and a *kind* to write to her family. Maybe if *Daed* explained why he'd sent back the letters, she could understand why he joyously had welcomed his granddaughter home while hardly acknowledging his daughter. There must be something more behind his actions than him being furious that she'd left with Johnny and his girlfriend, Carleen, years ago.

Wasn't there?

Ezra sensed the underlying anticipation in the members of the district who had gathered on the front lawn of Henry Gingerich's home. Part of today's worship included the selection of the new minister, and already the baptized members had nominated their choice for the next *Diener zum Buch* by whispering that man's name to the other minister or the bishop. Any married man whose name was whispered by three different members would be placed in the lot for the next "minister of the book," who would be expected to preach a sermon in two weeks and every other Sunday for the rest of his life.

The married men were gathered in small groups or stood with their wives and *kinder*. Everyone spoke in hushed voices, and, though nobody would be speculating on who would be called forward, he knew it was the main topic on everyone's mind.

He hoped the tension kept the rest of the congregation from noticing how his head snapped about when he heard Leah's lyrical voice not far from where he stood by himself. Looking to his right, he saw her with her arm around her niece's shoulders.

Since the day Mandy had named his pregnant Brown Swiss cow, he hadn't seen or spoken with either her or Leah. Amos had mentioned last night at supper that she had brought three beautiful quilts to the store earlier that day. His brother planned to display them close to the store's front door, so every customer would see them.

Ezra had no doubts that the quilts were extraordinary. Leah had been a skilled seamstress from the time she was her niece's age, and she always had been a welcome addition to any quilting frolic. Her eye for color, as well as her knowledge of fabrics and patterns, led to much older quilters asking for her advice.

But now she was busy talking in a low and steady voice to Mandy, who was shifting from one foot to the other. A rebellious expression on the girl's face warned she wasn't happy with whatever Leah said to her. Even though he knew he should stay away, that whatever Leah was talking about with Mandy was none of his business, he crossed the lawn to where they stood apart from the rest of the congregation.

"More?" Disbelief widened Mandy's dark blue eyes as he approached near enough to hear their low voices. "I thought, when we were sent outside, that we were done. When we went to church back home, it never lasted longer than an hour."

"A Communion Sunday always means a lengthier church service, and we need to have a minister selected, too."

"I wish we were back in Philadelphia."

"But then you wouldn't have met your *grossdawdi.*" Leah's attention was focused on her niece, so she didn't seem to see him come to stand behind her. "Usually church doesn't last this long. Once we're done, we'll eat and you can play with the other *kinder.*"

"Kinder?"

"Children."

"Oh, like in kindergarten."

Leah squeezed her niece's shoulders. "Exactly. You'll see when we have church again in two weeks what our services are usually like."

"They usually last about three hours," Ezra said as he aimed a smile at Leah and her niece.

Mandy grinned up at him. "Oh, hi, Mr. Stoltzfus!"

"Why don't you call me Ezra?" he corrected gently, not adding that the Amish didn't believe in using titles as *Englischers* did. Even their bishop was addressed by his given name, a reminder that all of them were equal in God's eyes. *"Gute mariye,* Leah."

"Good morning," she said, speaking English so Mandy wouldn't be shut out of their conversation. She didn't look at him. Instead she scanned the yard and the people gathered there. "Mandy, the selection of a new *Diener zum Buch* is fascinating, and it'll be better for everyone once the matter is settled."

He nodded. *"Ja."*

"Do you want to be chosen?" Mandy asked.

"I'm not wed. Only married men are in the lot to serve."

"Why?"

Wondering if the little girl pelted Leah with as many questions, he said, "Being a preacher is an important position with plenty of responsibility, so choosing from the married men who already have shown they can handle the responsibility of a family is—"

"No!" Mandy shook her head vehemently.

"You shouldn't interrupt," Leah chided, her voice soft but serious. "Most especially when someone is answering a question you've asked."

"But I'm not interested in why only married men can be ministers," the girl said with the logic of a nine-year-old.

"Then what do you want to know?"

Mandy looked up at Ezra and gave him an innocent grin. "I want to know why Ezra isn't married." She turned to Leah. "He's old, isn't he? I thought all old Amish men got married."

"He's only a few years older than I am," Leah said, a smile wafting along her lips.

Ezra saw that Leah's argument didn't change the little girl's mind. Leah was her *daed*'s twin, so for a *kind*, that could only mean that she was ancient, though she was not yet thirty. And she'd deemed him even more elderly.

To change the subject because it wasn't a topic he wanted to discuss during a break in the Sunday service, especially when Leah stood nearby, he said, "I see Abram is back from his trip. Did he have a successful time at the auction, Leah?"

"I—I don't know." Her smile fled from her face. "He didn't say, and I didn't have a chance to go out to the barn this morning."

He couldn't help wondering what had happened when Abram arrived home. A quick glance around the yard pinpointed Abram talking with several of the older men. Leah's *daed* scowled when one of the other men pointed toward where she and her niece stood with him. Though

Ezra couldn't hear what Abram said, from his motions and the other men's expressions, it was clear that his response was heated. Too heated for a church Sunday.

Ezra looked back at Leah and realized she'd been watching her *daed* and the other men, as well. Her chin was high, but she shook her head as she tried to keep the tears glistening in her eyes from tumbling down her cheeks.

The once-familiar yearning to pull her into his arms and protect her from the storms that filled her home rushed through him. In the past, the angry words had been between her twin and Abram, and the Stoltzfus family's barn had become a haven for her at least once a week. He had gotten accustomed to watching out the window to see her fleeing across the field, so he could be in the barn when she arrived. Though she never spoke of what was said between Johnny and her *daed*, their conversations on any other subject had lasted until she could put her distress behind her and slip back into her own house, which was silent in the wake of the quarrel.

That familiar yearning mixed with familiar frustration. Leah was the first to offer help, but accepting it from others was something she found impossible. If she had opened up to him about the tempests that blew through the Beiler household, maybe she could have turned to him and resisted Johnny's persuading her to leave Paradise Springs.

"Any animals Abram purchased," he hurried to say, wanting to bring her lighthearted expression back, "probably won't be delivered until next week or the week after."

Leah's smile returned but was as unsteady as a sapling in a storm.

"On Wednesday," Mandy piped up. "That's what he

told me when I was helping him get the buggy. He showed me how he hooks up the horse. I can't wait to tell Isabella about all I've learned once I get back home to Philadelphia."

Dismay dimmed Leah's eyes, and Ezra understood exactly why she was upset this time. She didn't want to lose her niece. Or would Leah go back to the city with Mandy if the little girl was unhappy here?

"Leah…" he began.

"Ezra…" she said at the same time.

When Mandy giggled, she said, "You're doing it again. Talking together."

"Go ahead," Leah urged.

"No. Ladies first. What were you about to say?"

She opened her mouth to answer, but closed it again as the Gingeriches' front door opened.

Reuben Lapp, their bishop, called from the porch, "We are ready."

As the congregation moved forward to retake their seats on the benches in the main room, Ezra sighed. Later, once the new minister was selected, he'd try to find some time to be alone with Leah. It was long past time for them to talk.

Really talk…just the two of them. He intended to find some time for that later today.

Chapter Five

Reuben Lapp stood with the district's deacon, Marlin Wagler, and their other preacher Atlee Bender in the center of the large room that was filled with backless benches. The gray-haired bishop with his impressive eyebrows and beard read the procedures for choosing the new preacher. Everyone in the room, save for the youngest *kinder*, were already familiar with them, and Reuben hurried through the reading. When he was finished, he didn't ask if anyone had any questions.

As Ezra listened, he fought to keep from looking—*again!*—at Leah, who sat behind his *mamm* and his sister-in-law Rose. Each time he saw Leah in a familiar setting like this, it was as if no time had passed since the night they had kissed by the stream. Yet so much time had elapsed, and so much had changed. His *daed* had died, and Ezra had taken over the farm while his brothers started businesses of their own. Two of his brothers and his older sister had married. Now he had nieces and nephews galore.

But Leah looked as fresh and lovely as she had before she left Paradise Springs. The time away had added a maturity to her steady gaze, but her cheeks had their youthful pink warmth. That soft color had been the very first thing he'd noticed when one day he found that he had stopped thinking of her as his best friend and had begun imagining asking if she'd agree for him to be her come-calling wooer.

She caught him looking at her, and a faint twinkle filled her eyes before she lowered her gaze. In that moment, the connection between them had been so strong that it seemed as if nobody else was in the room. He was relieved that she no longer looked humiliated, as she had when it was obvious Abram had been talking about her with some of the other members of the congregation.

He shouldn't be surprised. Leah Beiler was resilient. She'd proved that during her last couple of years in Paradise Springs when she sought sanctuary in his family's barn, away from the arguments between Abram and Johnny, more and more frequently. That she had lived for ten years among *Englischers* and was slipping back into the ways of a plain life with apparent ease were clearly two more examples of her ability to hold on to what was important to her.

"The following men are in the lot to serve this district as *Diener zum Buch*," Reuben said in his deep voice, which could resonate like a wild gust of wind through a room during an impassioned sermon.

Ezra heard the congregation draw in a breath as one. Nobody seemed to release it as Reuben picked up three copies of the *Ausbund*. That meant that three men would be called forward, and one among them would become the new minister. Within one of the hymnals, hidden so nobody could guess which book held it, was a piece of paper with verses written on it. The same verses were always used in their district, verses from the ninth chap-

ter of Luke explaining how Jesus gave his disciples the
duty to preach God's word.

*And He said unto them, Take nothing for your journey,
neither staves, nor scrip, neither bread, neither money...*

He glanced at his brother Joshua, who was already exhausted from working at his buggy shop and being a lone
parent to his *kinder*. Ezra couldn't imagine how Joshua
would find time in his full days to minister to the mem-
bership and to prepare to preach every other Sunday. His
brother-in-law Elmer Blauch and Ruth had seven *kinder*
as well as their farm, and he guessed Ruth might be pregnant again because her apron seemed to be growing taut
across her belly. Isaiah was a newlywed, married only
since last December, and he was trying to find a balance
between being a husband with his work at the smithy.

As his eyes swept the benches on the men's side of the
room, he knew none of the married men had time in their
busy lives to take on the duties of ministering to the *Leit*,
the people in their district. Yet, none of them would turn
down ordination as the next minister if chosen by the lot.

"Abram Beiler, come forward," Reuben said in the
thick silence.

Leah's *daed* stood and, without looking to his left or
right, went to sit on a bench at the front that had been
left empty for the ordination. His fingers shook, but his
face was set in a stern expression.

A single glance at where Leah sat on the bench behind
Mamm's reminded Ezra that Abram had no son to help
him with the family's farm. If Abram was selected as the
new preacher, he would likely need to hire a boy or two to
assist in planting and harvesting. Perhaps Ezra's nephew
Timothy would be interested because, so far, the boy had
shown little interest in following in Joshua's footsteps and

learning the steps for making a buggy or repairing one. He worked at the buggy shop but did only the most basic tasks like sanding or painting.

Reuben waited for Abram to sit, then announced, "Isaiah Stoltzfus, come forward."

Ezra heard a soft cry, quickly muffled from the women's benches. Rose, Isaiah's wife, hid her face in her hands. Leah put her hand on Rose's shoulder while *Mamm* whispered to his sister-in-law. He guessed they both were trying to calm her. He sighed. Not only could the weight of a minister's duties on top of his ones to his family and job be massive, but the expectations placed on a minister's wife could be onerous, as well. She must become a role model for the other women in the district, living her life and raising her family in the public eye. For a couple who had been married such a short time and were still learning to live as husband and wife, the burden would be even more difficult.

Even as Isaiah moved to sit beside Abram, Reuben said, "Henry Gingerich, come forward."

The man, whose family was hosting the service, was almost a decade older than Abram. He glanced at his wife, who pressed her fingers over her mouth, but walked toward the front. Was she as astonished as Ezra that her elderly husband had been included in the lot? Henry was a *gut* man, and clearly at least three of the *Leit* had deemed him worthy of being their next preacher.

Ezra tried to concentrate on the prayer he should be sending up to God for wisdom for the man chosen to be their next minister. It wasn't easy to think of wisdom when he felt sorry for Rose. Her soft sobs came from the other side of the room. He tried not to be angry with God for allowing troubles into the lives of those who loved

Him. God could see the entire world and how each piece fit together, but the frustration he'd felt when he learned of Leah leaving with her brother returned doubly strong. Was his faith so fragile that any bump in the path he was walking gave him pause? He'd asked himself that question ten years ago and gotten no answer. Now he was asking it again.

No one spoke as Reuben set the three books on a table and stepped aside. One at a time, in the order they'd been called, the three men rose and selected a book. Reuben moved in front of the men who knelt. He held out his hand to Abram, who handed him the book. Reuben riffled through the pages, but no piece of paper fell out.

Isaiah was next. He offered the *Ausbund* to the bishop. Reuben opened the hymnbook and raised it to display the piece of paper stuck between two pages written in German.

Before either man could speak, Rose jumped to her feet. "No! No! No!" she shrieked. "No, not Isaiah! Please, God, no!"

Everyone froze, including Abram and Henry, who had been coming to their feet.

Everyone except Leah, who stood and put her hand on Rose's shoulder again. Through Rose's cries, she said in a steady, calm voice as she stepped over the bench where *Mamm* sat in astonishment, "It will be all right, Rose. It will be."

Rose threw herself toward Leah, who embraced her gently and let her sob against her neck. Guiding the weeping Rose along the bench, Leah steered her toward the closest door, as if Rose were a fussy baby who was carried outside to be kept from disrupting the service.

Ezra started to rise, then halted and sat again when he

caught sight of Isaiah's face. His brother was clearly torn between his new obligations and his overwrought wife. Yet, Isaiah didn't come to his feet as he readied himself to accept the duties and burden of serving God and the members of their district.

Leah reached the door to what he knew was a downstairs bedroom and opened it. Over his sister-in-law's head, her gaze met Ezra's. He saw both the sympathy and determination in her eyes. As always, Leah was ready to jump to the assistance of anyone who needed her.

His jaw tightened. Even though he should be grateful that she'd stepped forward to help Rose, the alacrity was a sure sign that Leah hadn't changed. He had known she was being honest when she explained she'd gone with Johnny in order to try to persuade him to come home. Hadn't she learned that she should look before she leaped?

Instantly he chided himself. Leah offering Rose solace was completely different than running off to Philadelphia with her brother.

Wasn't it?

He was dismayed to discover that he was no longer sure.

Leah sat at a picnic table not far from the kitchen door, hand sewing patches together for a quilt top. The pattern eventually would become the one called Sunshine and Shadow. Even though the spring breeze gusted and tried to sweep the fabric out of her hands, she enjoyed piecing together the variety of squares into a great diamond pattern, though she would do the wider borders on her *mamm*'s treadle sewing machine. The style sold well for the quilts she'd consigned to Mrs. Whittaker's antique shop in Philadelphia. She hoped her quilts would sell as well at Amos Stoltzfus's store in Paradise Springs. One of the quilts she'd delivered to him was also in the Sunshine and Shadow pattern, but she could not wait to see how long it took to sell if she wanted to have more quilts finished to bring to his shop.

As her needle darted in and out of the cotton in small, even stitches, she gazed around the yard. Everyone had been well fed after the long service came to a close. The adults now were gathered again in small groups, and she guessed most of them were carefully *not* talking about the results of the lot. As far as she knew, Rose remained in the house, lying down in a darkened room, as her *mamm* and sisters joined Isaiah in trying to help her see that, though her life would change, it didn't have to be for the worse.

Her smile returned when she saw Mandy running about the yard with a few of the other girls her age. She was giggling and obviously having a *gut* time. Maybe she would come to love living in Paradise Springs and stop talking about returning to Philadelphia as if the decision had already been made. Leah didn't want to make her niece feel like a prisoner in Lancaster County, but the idea of losing Mandy was as painful as losing Johnny.

Leah's thoughts were yanked away from her niece when she noticed Ezra striding toward the picnic table where she sat. Though he had glanced her way too often during the service, she hadn't seen him since it was over. She guessed he'd eaten with the other men while the women readied food for themselves and the *kinder* in the kitchen. By the time she'd left Rose, knowing she could do no more for Isaiah's wife, she'd been grateful to find a plate of food waiting for her on the kitchen table.

Ezra leaned one hand on the picnic table. His wide fingers were calloused from hard work, but she couldn't remember them ever looking different. As long as she'd known him, he'd worked in the barn, eager to learn all he could about cows and farming. Unlike her brother, who always wanted to see what was beyond the next hill, Ezra had never wanted to be anything but a farmer and a cheese-maker.

"You look deep in thought." His face was creased with lines she hadn't seen before. Having the lot fall on Isaiah, and Rose's reaction, were difficult for both the Stoltzfus and Mast families.

"I think everyone is, including you." She lowered her sewing to her lap.

"*Ja.* Do you want to know what I'm thinking?"

"Sure."

"I'm thinking that it isn't going to be easy to have my naughty, impish little brother Isaiah as our new preacher."

She smiled at his wry expression. "You'd better get used to the idea. The duties have been laid upon him, and he will do well."

"You sound very certain of that." He crossed his arms over his chest, which had broadened during her years away. He had taken off his *Mutze*, the black coat men wore to church services, and his suspenders were dark against his white shirt.

"I can't imagine any of Paul and Wanda Stoltzfus's *kinder* not giving anything they do less than one hundred percent of their effort."

For a long moment, he stared at her without replying before he said, *"Danki."*

"There is no need to thank me for speaking the truth."

"Let me be honest, too, and say that I came over here

wondering if you'd agree if I asked you to go for a walk with me. Henry mentioned something to me that I think you'll find very interesting."

"What?"

He tapped her nose as he had when they were kids and said, "Curiosity killed the cat."

"I'm not a cat."

"I've noticed that."

Looking away from his abruptly serious gaze, Leah was suffused with a warmth that was both delightful and unsettling. She should come up with a reason to turn down his offer gently. To walk away with Ezra would be paramount to announcing to everyone gathered there that they were courting. Yet, he was right. She was curious what Henry had told Ezra that she would find intriguing. And, though she was reluctant to mention it even to herself, she liked the idea of having time with Ezra.

Leah put her quilting into a small bag, then set it on the table. The breeze was stiffening, but it wasn't strong enough to send her bag tumbling to the ground. As she came to her feet, Ezra's smile broadened. A pulse of happiness danced through her. His smile had always done that to her, even when they were little kids.

He motioned for her to follow as they walked toward where the teens were playing softball. It was the favorite sport in their district, and some of the younger teenage girls had joined in while the older ones watched and whispered about the boys. She could remember when she had played softball, and she recalled how her friends had spoken quietly of crushes on Ezra. She had listened to them, but she'd never thought of him as a boy she could have a crush on. He was her best friend, even closer in some ways than her twin brother, especially once Johnny reached *rumspringa* age.

Then came the night when Ezra kissed her, and everything changed. Again she wondered, as she had many times, what would have happened if she'd had a chance to ask Ezra about the wondrous kiss. She'd imagined him saying many different things when she asked if he'd intended to kiss her, but the time to ask him was long past.

As they passed the ball game, both teams of teens burst into shouts of excitement as two ran around the bases while an outfielder chased the ball. It rolled toward Ezra. He picked it up and threw it to the boy who'd raced after it. As the boy yelled "*danki*," Ezra turned toward a path leading along the edge of a field. He gave her a brash grin.

"What?" she asked when he didn't speak.

"No comments on my precision throw?"

"Pride isn't *gut*, and fishing for compliments can leave you with nothing for your efforts."

He opened the gate. "To the point, as always."

"*Ja.* I try to be."

"Then I'll get right to the point and say I didn't expect to see you climbing over a bench today during the lot."

"I suppose you think that is silly."

"No." He became serious as he let her step around the open gate first. "I think you were very kind to step in and help Rose. The rest of us were too shocked to do anything, but you helped her. I guess some things and some people don't change."

She frowned at him but kept walking. "Why are you acting like this? First you say you're glad I could offer Rose some comfort. With the next breath, you make it sound like a bad thing."

Taking off his black hat, he ran his hand through his hair. Several strands stood out at odd angles before he set his hat back on his head again. "That isn't what I meant."

"What did you mean?"

He raised his hands in a pose of surrender as he shrugged. "I'm honestly not sure what I meant. You haven't changed, Leah, in your determination to help people. That's a *gut* thing, right?"

"I think so."

"*Gut*. Me, too. Can you forget I said everything I said but that I appreciate you helping Rose?"

"I was glad I could help a little bit." Would he notice that she hadn't answered his question? "Rose will come to accept God's will."

"I pray you are right."

"God gives us nothing we can't handle as long as we depend on Him to guide the way."

"I would like to think that."

She glanced at him, startled. Had Ezra's faith faltered while she was away? Dismay clamped tightly around her heart. She had always admired his strong assurance in God's close walk with them. Now...she was unsure what to think.

They strolled along in silence to the far end of the field. At the gate there, Ezra turned and looked back at the large white house with its *dawdi haus* attached to one side. Some buggies were already pulling away from where they'd been parked by the large whitewashed stone barn.

"Henry has been interested in the results I'm getting with the Brown Swiss herd," he said as if they'd been talking of nothing else, "and he's thinking about starting his own herd. He says as long as he can't sell his milk for a decent price to the bottling plant, he should consider cows that give milk with a higher cream content."

She nodded, though she was curious at how he suddenly changed the subject. Maybe he was right. They had been wandering into very personal territory, and it was better not to do that.

Leah rested one arm on the metal rail at the top of the gate and stared at the farm buildings, too. She knew Henry had decided not to put a refrigerated tank in his barn. With the milk being kept cool in cans that he set in water pumped from the deep pond behind his barn, the only place he could sell it was to a cheese-making plant.

"Does he want to make cheese on the farm as you do?" she asked.

"I don't think he's thought that far ahead yet. You know Henry. A chicken cowering in the coop to evade a fox isn't any more cautious than Henry is about making a move."

"But won't his youngest son take over the farm soon?"

"Lemuel wants to, but Henry can't let go of the reins." He grabbed the latch on the gate and lifted it. "C'mon. What I want to show you is this way."

As Leah stepped past the open gate, a gust of wind swirled around them. She clapped her hand on the black bonnet she wore over her *kapp*. Her *kapp* strings snapped out to the side. She caught them before they could strike Ezra in the face, but the back of her hand brushed against his cheek.

Heat seemed to leap from his skin to hers. She froze, unable to move in any direction, as his warmth coursed through her. Memories she'd tried to bury flooded her. She jerked her hand back and turned her head so she couldn't see his expression. She didn't want to know if he'd felt that spark like flint on steel, too.

But his voice had a raw edge to it, as if something was stuck in his throat...or he was trying not to say what he really wanted to say. "Let's go." He stepped around her and strode toward a thicket of trees.

She started to follow, then stopped, realizing they were walking in the direction of the stream where he had kissed her. Going there would be foolish. What had happened that night was so long ago it seemed like someone else's life, not hers. Yet she could recall his gentle lips and the way his breath had tasted of the soda he'd brought for them to share.

"It's just a little farther," he said, pointing to the left.

The spot on the stream where he'd kissed her was to the right. Maybe he didn't even remember that night, which remained special for her. For all she knew, he'd kissed plenty of other girls since she went away with Johnny. Just because she hadn't looked at another man with interest—not even the few plain men she'd met at the Reading Terminal Market in the heart of Philadelphia— didn't mean that Ezra hadn't spent time with other women. Maybe he even had a special one now.

When Leah stepped past the trees, she stared at a pond she didn't recall. Then she saw what appeared to be a pile of tree debris that had clogged the stream, creating the pool of water.

"It's a beaver dam!" she exclaimed. "How long has it been here?"

"A couple of years. Shortly after they built it, the water began backing up into this pond. Around the same time, the bank collapsed out along the edge of our fields." He put his finger to his lips and whispered, "Listen."

Leah strained her ears. She could hear only the wind's murmured song and her own breathing. Holding her breath, she released it slowly as she heard what sounded like mewing kittens hidden in the trees on the far side of the pond.

When she said that, he nodded. "You're hearing a litter of beaver kits inside the dam. Even though their parents sleep during the day, they're awake day and night like human babies. And like human babies, they cry when they're hungry. Let's go before *daed* and *mamm* beaver hear us."

"All right. *Danki* for bringing me here. I—" Her voice caught as his hand cupped her elbow. Every word she knew raced out of her head. Time collapsed to the moment when he'd held her that one night and kissed her. Then she'd been little more than a *kind*. Now she was a grown-up woman, and she must not make the same mistake again.

When he turned her to face him, they stood so close she was aware of every breath he took. Was that his heart pounding or hers? She started to close her eyes as his fingers rose to stroke her cheek; then she pulled away. No, she *must* not make the same mistake again.

Ezra knew the instant he touched Leah that he was being foolish. His plan had been to ask her out to the pond to see the beaver dam as an excuse to get her alone so he could ask if she planned to stay in Paradise Springs or return to Philadelphia as her niece seemed to expect. Now, none of that seemed to matter as much as his yearning to bring her into his arms.

Before he could let that temptation completely overwhelm him, she had drawn away and was walking back toward the farmhouse. He matched her steps but took care not to let even her skirt hem brush against him as he held the gate for her again. She said nothing, and he didn't know how to bridge the abrupt chasm between them.

Back at the house, she hurried to join her parents and Mandy in the family buggy. He considered waving as it drove away, but she didn't look in his direction as she spoke with her niece.

You made a complete mess of that.

Ezra sighed as the chiding thought bounced through his mind. He leaned his shoulder against a tree and looked across the fields toward the western sky where the bright red color of the clouds closest to the horizon forecasted fine weather tomorrow. It would be the perfect day to begin the first cut of hay in the field on the far side of the barn. Usually he couldn't wait for the spring day when he hooked up the mules and headed out into the lush grass. The fresh, green scent of the scythed hay was as sweet and heady as the aroma of watermelon rind on a hot summer day.

But he couldn't imagine losing himself in the pleasure of being out in the sunshine and quenching his thirst on *Mamm*'s lemonade. Not when his thoughts were topsy-turvy.

Not just his thoughts, but his life.

Chapter Six

The next morning, as Leah helped Mandy twist her braids into place for her first day at school, she couldn't keep Ezra out of her mind. She should never have gone for that walk with him. Oh, how she wished she could go back to the time when she and Ezra were best friends and they could say anything to each other without worrying about a misunderstanding! Then he could put his hand on her arm, and it was nothing more than the amiable connection between two people who'd grown up next door to each other.

"Ouch!" complained Mandy. "You pulled my hair."

"I'm sorry." She loosened her grip on the braid. She'd become wound up and hadn't noticed that she'd tightened her hold on it.

Suddenly sharp barking came from downstairs. A loud thump reverberated. She exchanged a glance with Mandy in the mirror, then tossed the brush on the freshly made bed. Her niece was right on her heels as she raced down the back stairs and into the kitchen.

She stared. *Daed* sat at the table, his hand pressed to his forehead. Blood seeped between his fingers. More crimson was streaked across the edge of the table. *Mamm* stood by the stove, the oatmeal ladle in one hand, the fingers of her other hand pressed over her mouth.

Without a word, Leah ran into the bathroom and got the first-aid kit. She opened it as she returned. Pulling out squares of gauze *Mamm* kept in the small metal box for times like this one, she shoved the box into Mandy's hands. She offered the bottle of iodine and the gauze to *Mamm*, who shook herself out of her shock. Her *mamm* put down the ladle and stepped around the oatmeal that had dropped in thick globs onto the floor.

"Danki," Mamm said as she asked *Daed* to lower his hand so she could clean the blood away enough to allow her to examine the cut on his forehead.

"What happened to *Grossdawdi*?" asked Mandy, fear sifting into her voice.

"Let's get your *grossdawdi* fixed up first before we ask questions." Leah smiled gently at her niece as she added, "Will you keep these supplies close by, so we have what we need?"

"Ja."

Leah was startled at Mandy's reply, but the girl had begun using other *Deitsch* words. Was it a sign her niece was willing to stay in Paradise Springs? *God, please help me show her that her place is here with her family.*

Her prayer was cut short when *Daed* yelped. She remembered when *Mamm* had used iodine on scrapes and small cuts she and her sisters and brother had ended up with after climbing trees or playing ball. It always stung.

Shep rushed around the table and sat beside Leah. She glanced at him, astonished. With the raised voices and tension in the kitchen, she'd expected he would continue barking and running around the room. Glad that he was behaving, she reached down to pat his silky head, and he lapped her hand quickly with his smooth tongue before giving her a proud doggie grin.

She recognized his actions. He'd learned them as part of his service dog training. Why was he acting as if he'd used his skills this morning? Maybe he believed he'd alerted her to *Daed*'s accident as he had to Johnny's seizures.

Before she could give it much more thought, her *daed* said, "Enough! I am fine. I don't need you fussing around me, Fannie."

"You are not fine!" *Mamm* argued. "You stumbled hard, and you've got a lump the size of an egg on your forehead, as well as that cut. Fortunately, it isn't very deep. For once, your hard head served you well."

He started to reply, then winced. He remained silent while *Mamm* worked. When she stepped back, a small white bandage was taped over his left eye.

Mandy rushed to her *grossdawdi* and took his right hand in hers. He withdrew it, then grasped her hand with his left one.

"Are you all right, *Grossdawdi*?" she asked.

"Your *grossmammi* is right. I have a hard head. I'm fine."

"But it must hurt."

"Maybe it's God's way of reminding me to be more careful and watch where I step."

Leah bit her lip as she heard how gentle her *daed* was with Mandy. Even if he hardly spoke to Leah, he had welcomed his granddaughter without hesitation. The little girl needed their love and patience as she became accustomed to living a plain life. Yet… Leah couldn't help wishing that *Daed* would show her the same little signs of affection.

"But what happened?" Mandy's question shredded Leah's moment of self-pity.

Just as well, because she had no right to feel sorry for herself. Nor should she blame *Daed* for being angry with her. Leah had broken her parents' hearts when she vanished along with Johnny. She'd betrayed their trust in her to make the correct decision and to hold tight to what she knew was right. That she had made every effort to live a plain life in Philadelphia meant nothing to them. Somehow, she must earn her *daed*'s forgiveness for her foolish hopes that she could bring Johnny to his senses.

"It was that dog." *Daed* pointed at Shep. "He was barking like he'd lost every sensible thought in his little head. When he jumped in front of me, I tried to move aside. I tripped over him. I don't know why you had to bring that foolish creature here. He doesn't belong in this house."

"Because he's my daddy's dog!" cried Mandy, yanking her hand out of his. She ran over to the dog and scooped him up. With him held close to her heart, she moaned. "Shep is the only thing I've got left that belonged to my daddy. If you make him go away like you made Daddy go away, I'm going, too." She burst into tears. "I wish we'd never left Philadelphia. I want to go home. Leah, can't we go home?"

Putting her arms around her niece, Leah leaned her head against the top of Mandy's. She saw her parents' shocked expressions. She wondered exactly what Johnny had told his daughter about why he and Leah had left Paradise Springs. They'd had plenty of time to talk while she was out of the apartment, running errands. Whatever Johnny had revealed hadn't soured the relationship

Mandy had begun to build with *Daed*, but clearly he'd said enough for his daughter to know that he hadn't been happy while he lived in his parents' house.

Leah forced a happy lilt in her voice, hoping that it didn't sound as insincere as it felt. "Today isn't a day to go to Philadelphia. It's a day to go to school. Why don't you put Shep down and give him some milk?"

"But if they make him go away like they did Daddy—"

"*Grossdawdi* is hurt, and when we're hurt, we can be angry and say things we don't mean. Like you did when you dropped the iron on your big toe last summer."

Mandy nodded but didn't raise her head or release the dog.

"Why don't we have our breakfast now?" Leah added in her far too perky voice. "You don't want to be late for school."

"But Shep—"

"He'll be waiting for you when you come home." *Mamm* put her hands on Mandy's shoulders and turned her toward the table. "Come and sit. Your breakfast is getting cold."

"You'll give Shep some eggs, *Grossmammi*?" Mandy asked.

"*Ja*, and maybe a bite or two of sausage."

That brought a smile to the little girl, and as quickly as that, it appeared all was forgiven. Leah hoped that was true.

As soon as Mandy was perched on her chair, Leah and *Mamm* took their own. They prayed in silence, then began eating. Mandy remained subdued in spite of *Mamm*'s efforts to draw her out.

Leah was never so glad to be done with a meal. After

finishing her hair and setting her *kapp* on her head, Leah went to pick up her bonnet off the peg by the back door.

Mandy petted Shep's head, told him to be a *gut* dog and ran outside to climb into the waiting buggy that was set to go. As soon as she left the room, *Daed* dropped his face into his hands. He gave a groan, but Leah couldn't guess if Mandy's words or banging his head against the table hurt him more. Beside him, *Mamm* was struggling not to cry. He said only that he'd be out in the barn as he pushed himself to his feet. His steps grew steadier as he walked to the back door, but his hands continued to shake.

"I'm sorry, *Mamm*," Leah said as silence settled on the kitchen again. "It hurts to see your face when Mandy talks about going back to the city. Each time, it's another reminder of how I caused you and *Daed* such pain by leaving like I did. It hurts me, too, but I can understand why God would punish me. I don't understand why He would punish you because of my stupid mistakes."

Mamm put her hands on either side of Leah's face. Compassion filled her eyes as she said, "My dear *kind*, you know that isn't how God is. We live according to His will, but He doesn't punish us when we make mistakes. He loves us, in spite of our human failings, and He wants us to learn from our mistakes."

"I'm trying to."

"I know you are." She kissed Leah's cheek, then stepped back. "Hurry and get Mandy to school, or she'll be late on her very first day there. Don't forget to ask Esther how her family is doing today."

"*Daed*—"

"I'll keep an eye on him and on Shep. Stop worrying, Leah. It'll be fine."

Leah wished she shared her *mamm*'s optimism. After she tied her black bonnet under her chin, she went outside. She heard Shep's anxious whine when she shut the door, but she didn't want to make it a habit to have the dog in the buggy. *Daed* had already complained about cleaning dog hair off the seats.

She had a smile firmly in place by the time she climbed into the buggy and sat next to Mandy. Feeling the smooth rhythm of the horse's gait through the reins and listening to the whir of metal wheels on the asphalt as they turned onto the road soothed Leah. She'd become accustomed to taking a bus, and the crowded, noisy, smoke-belching vehicle hadn't been as satisfying as the steady clip-clop.

She glanced at Mandy, who was chewing on one of her *kapp* strings. Gently, Leah drew it out of her hand and let it fall back against her niece's new black dress. Like Leah, Mandy would wear only black dresses and capes for the next year as they mourned for Johnny.

"Maybe I should go another day," Mandy said in little more than a whisper. "I'm sorry I upset *Grossdawdi*. I need to tell him that."

"He'll be glad to hear your apology after school."

"I've never been the new kid in school before. What if they don't like me?"

Leah stroked her niece's arm. "How could they *not* like you? And it's not like there will be only strangers there. Esther Stoltzfus will be your teacher."

"I like Esther. She makes *gut* cookies."

"You know her niece Deborah Stoltzfus," she said, hiding her smile at Mandy's response, "and I saw you playing with the younger Burkholder girls—Anna and

Joyce—at church yesterday. I suspect you already know all the girls who sit in your row in the school."

"That's only three!"

"Someone mentioned there are twenty scholars attending school this year." She smiled. "That's what we call the *kinder* who are in school. Scholars. You are a scholar now, too."

"There are only twenty kids in my class?"

Leah shook her head, realizing anew how great the changes were that her niece was facing. When Leah had arrived in Philadelphia, she had been astounded at every turn by the ways that were different in the city. She had gratefully left, bringing Mandy with her, without understanding that the life they lived in Paradise Springs would be almost as alien to the little girl as the city had been for Leah. Some things Mandy knew about because Leah had tried to live a plain life even in the city, but how much did the little girl truly comprehend?

"There are twenty scholars," she said in the gentle voice she'd found worked best with Mandy when pointing out differences in their lives in Paradise Springs, "in the whole school."

"Only twenty kids from kindergarten to twelfth grade?"

"Our scholars attend school only until the eighth grade."

Mandy's scowl depended. "Then they go to high school in the village? Isn't that the big brick building we passed when we went to drop off your quilts at the grocery store?"

"Yes, that's the *Englisch* school, but Amish scholars don't go there."

"Then where do they go?"

"After eighth grade, our *kinder* take an apprentice-ship, learning a trade or working beside their parents on the farm."

"But I don't want to be a farmer or a…a p-p-prentice." She flushed as she fought to say the unfamiliar word.

Leah quickly explained what an apprentice was. "Deb-orah's older brother Timothy works as an apprentice at his *daed*'s buggy shop."

"But I want to be a nurse."

"You do?" Leah was sure she hadn't heard Mandy talk about that before.

"*Ja*, and how can I get to be a nurse if I don't go to college? When I asked a couple of Daddy's nurses and physical therapists about doing what they did when I grew up, they told me that the best thing I could do was go to college to learn everything I need to know. They thought I would make a *gut* nurse. Daddy thought so, too."

Leah was shocked into silence by how her niece mixed *Deitsch* words with *Englisch* plans for her future. She sent up a silent prayer of gratitude when the schoolhouse came into view. That saved her from having to find an answer to Mandy's comments.

At the sight of the small, white building with two win-dows on each side and a porch on the front, her niece hunched back against the seat as if she could make her-self too small to be seen by the scholars playing on the swings. Others ran around where the ground was worn from their ball games.

Leah turned the buggy onto the road that led to the school. She halted it under a tree. In front of them, an-other smaller building with a pair of doors was the out-house. A propane tank was set away from the school, but its brightly colored flexible pipes snaked to the building and the single stove that kept the scholars warm. Neither the stove nor the kerosene lamps that hung from the ceiling inside would be needed now that spring had banished the winter's cold and early darkness.

A shadow moved on the roof, and she realized someone was up there working. The winter had been harsh and the snow heavy, so some of the shingles might have come loose when the snow was shoveled off to keep the roof from capsizing.

Her attention was caught by two girls who were running toward the buggy. She saw they were Deborah Stoltzfus and Anna Burkholder. They shouted for Mandy to come and join them on the swings.

Looking up at Leah with fearful eyes, Mandy whispered, "You'll come with me, won't you, Aunt Leah?"

"*Ja*. Today."

The little girl looked ready to protest, but she quickly acquiesced and jumped out of the buggy.

Following, Leah lashed the reins to the hitching post, and then she held out her hand to Mandy, who clutched it as if it were a life preserver.

Esther came out on the porch and pulled the rope hooked to the bell by the door. Its clang, which muffled the sound of enthusiastic hammering up on the roof, was the signal that the school day was about to begin. The *kinder* were laughing and teasing each other as they ran to line up at the base of the porch steps. Leah knew that upon entering the school they would place their insulated lunch boxes on the shelves above the pegs for their hats and coats.

"Mandy," Esther said as Leah led her niece up the steps, "I'm glad you are joining us. Today you can watch and listen and see how we do things. I think you'll find we're not that different from *Englisch* schools."

"Aunt Leah?" The little girl gave her a frantic look and tightened her hold on Leah's hand.

"Your *aenti* is welcome to join us for a short time." Esther slid her arm around Mandy's shoulders. "Why don't you both come with me, and I'll show you where you will be sitting? Our other fourth-grade girls have been looking forward to having you join them."

Mandy's head swiveled as they walked into the single room, but for Leah, it was like stepping back in time. She had spent eight years there. The blackboards at the front of the room behind the teacher's desk didn't seem quite as high as she remembered. Each desk had a chair hooked to the front for the scholar in the next row. The same darkly stained wainscoting covered the walls beneath the windows, and similar posters, urging *gut* study habits and outlining the values that were central to their community, hung on the walls. Only the potbellied stove at the front was different.

As soon as Mandy was seated at a desk with Deborah on one side and Joyce Burkholder on the other with Anna Burkholder right behind her, Esther went to the front of the room. She picked up her well-worn Bible and opened it to the Book of Luke and read the parable of the lost sheep, the story of how heaven rejoices when a single lost lamb returns to the flock.

Leah wondered if Esther had chosen it especially for her and Mandy. Hearing that familiar parable beneath the steady hammering on the roof made her feel welcome. It must have done the same for her niece because Mandy was holding both of her friends' hands when the *kinder* rose to sing their morning song. Again, whether by chance or not, it was "Jesus Loves Me," a song she'd taught Mandy.

The *kinder* opened their workbooks and bent over them. Mandy leaned across the aisle to look at Deborah's. Leah murmured a prayer of gratitude that her niece was fitting in well and quickly.

Esther came to the back of the room where Leah stood. "She's going to do fine."

"I hope so."

"Then why do you look as uneasy as she did when she arrived?"

Lowering her voice and turning her back so none of the scholars could discern her words, Leah said, "Mandy told me she wants to go to college to be a nurse. I didn't know what to say to her. She has faced many changes already, and I want her to be as happy as possible." Her voice threatened to break when she added, "Johnny told her that he thought she'd make a *gut* nurse, so now she sees the choice in part as a tribute to him."

Esther put a gentle hand on Leah's arm. "If you want my advice…"

"*Ja*, I do," she replied, though she couldn't help finding it strange to be seeking the advice from someone who had been Mandy's age the last time Leah lived in Paradise Springs.

"My advice is do nothing but listen when she talks about her plans. There is nothing else you can do now other than what you've already been doing by being a *gut* example for her. She has this year and four more at this school. When I was nine, I was sure I wanted to join the circus and ride around the ring on white horses like the ones I read about in some storybook I picked up at the market in Lancaster while *Mamm* was selling cookies and *Daed*'s wooden shelves that the *Englischers* loved." She smiled, her eyes crinkling as Ezra's did.

Leah hadn't seen Ezra's smile enough since her return. Now and then, but mostly he was somber around her. More than she'd expected, she missed the ease they'd once shared.

As she reached for the doorknob, she said, "I should go. I've taken up too much of your time already."

"The *kinder* are doing their silent reading." She glanced up as the hammer struck the roof again. "Or almost silent reading. He should be finished soon."

"Oh, *Mamm* wanted to know how your family is doing," Leah said as she opened the door.

"If you mean Isaiah and Rose, he stopped by this morning on his way to work to let us know she is calmer today."

"I'm glad to hear that."

"If you mean Ezra…"

"I know he's worried about Isaiah and Rose," she quickly said.

"And you're worried about him?" Esther didn't give her a chance to answer. "I am, too. I'm sure you can see the changes in him."

"Ten years is a long time."

"Truc, but even those of us who have been here all along can see that Ezra isn't like he was before…*Daed* died."

Had she been going to say *since you left*? Leah couldn't be sure, and she was glad Esther had chosen the words she had.

"How is he different?" she asked.

"Unless he's with one of us, he spends all his time working on the farm. Not just chores, but working on his plans to create several flavors of cheese that he can sell at the farmer's market in Bird-in-Hand. He's not interested in anything else."

"That's enough to keep him busy."

"*Ja*, but it's more than that. Joshua joined the Paradise Springs Fire Department years ago. When Amos and Jeremiah joined, they asked Ezra to volunteer along with them. He's always calm in an emergency, so they knew he'd make a *gut* firefighter. He said he didn't have time for the training. When we were *kinder, he* used to talk about volunteering with the fire department as soon as he could."

"I remember."

The first time he mentioned it, she had urged him to consider it seriously. Being a volunteer fireman would enable him to help others, and, at the time, doing that had seemed as important to him as it was to her.

"And you know what the oddest thing is?" Esther went on as if Leah hadn't spoken. "When the fire department began talking about raising money for more training for their volunteers, Ezra offered our barn. He didn't wait to be asked. He told Amos and Jeremiah to let the fire chief know that they could use our barn for the mud sale that's being held next Saturday. The field in front of it would be fallow this year, so tables could be set up there to sell food and whatever else anyone had to sell as long as some of the money was donated to the fire department. I had hoped, once I heard you were back…" She clamped her lips closed and looked past Leah toward the door.

At the same moment, Leah heard, "Esther, I…"

As Ezra's voice trailed away, Leah faced him. His light brown hair was plastered to his brow by sweat. Though she and Esther had been talking about how he'd changed from the boy he'd been, there was no question that he was a man. He wore the sweat of a man's honest labor on his forehead, and the square line of his jaw tightened as their gazes collided and held.

She broke that link as she recalled how his sister and the scholars were watching. "I didn't realize the person up on the roof was you, Ezra."

"My big brother has been kind enough to do small repairs around the school." Esther's smile seemed strained, and Leah guessed Esther had sensed the unspoken tension between her and her brother. "The farm is closer than my other brothers' shops in Paradise Springs, so he's the one I call." She laughed, but the sound was as taut as her expression.

"The roof shingles are secure," he said in a flat voice. "You shouldn't have any more water leaking through the ceiling. But if you do, send one of the scholars for me immediately." He shoved the hammer in his belt and turned toward the front door. "See you later."

Before she quite realized what she was doing, Leah followed him outside. She closed the door behind her, then spoke his name.

He stepped off the porch but glanced back over his shoulder in surprise. She was shocked, too, that she had chased after him, but what she had to say needed to be said straightaway.

Coming down the steps until her eyes were level with his, she said, "Ezra, *danki* for stopping."

"I know you. You would chase after me until I did stop and listen to what you have to say." There was a hint of humor in his voice, but he tipped his hat so she didn't have as clear a view of his face.

She considered moving down another step so he

couldn't hide his expression from her. She resisted. They weren't *kinder* having an argument over whether a ball had been fair or foul. They were two people who were trying to find their way through a maze that seemed to have no discernible pattern.

"What I have to say, Ezra, is that we need to make it clear to everyone how we understand it's not easy for anyone, including ourselves, to know how to act after all this time. We can't have everyone around us acting as if they're walking on eggshells."

"I'm not sure what you expect me to do to change other people's perceptions."

"I expect you to stop behaving like Mandy does when she can't get her way."

Ezra swallowed his gasp of surprise at Leah's sharp words. He saw the flash of dismay on her face and knew something was bothering her. Something more than his terse words inside the school. Was it because he'd overstepped yesterday by the beaver pond? She had every right to be upset with him when she'd trusted him enough to walk with him through the woods.

"Ezra, I'm sorry," she said before he could find the words to defuse the situation.

"Don't apologize," he said with a sigh. "You are right. I'm acting like a *boppli*."

"No, you aren't acting like a baby." She stepped down to the ground, and he moved aside to leave space between them. "It's wrong of me to take out my uncertainty on you."

When she walked toward her family's buggy, he followed. There was much that needed to be said between them, but he wasn't sure where to begin. He suspected she felt the same, because she didn't say anything until she reached the buggy.

"Don't let Esther dump her silly worries on you," he said.

She turned to face him, and he saw his disquiet mirrored on her pretty face. "They aren't silly. You *have* changed."

"I should hope so. I was a foolish kid the last time you saw me. I would hope I'm a little less foolish now." He shook his head as he fought his fingers that wanted to slip around her slender waist and guide her into his arms. "It seems that I'm as *dumm* as I've always been."

"No, you aren't stupid, but something is clearly wrong. What is it?"

For the briefest second, he considered telling her that the first thing he thought of in the morning was holding her. The last thing he saw at night before he fell asleep was an image of her smile. Until he knew for sure that she wasn't leaving again, he couldn't risk his battered heart again.

"One of my cows is acting strangely," he replied. It was the other worry on his mind.

"Mamm Millich?"

He nodded with a sigh, not a bit astonished that she had guessed the truth easily. She knew some aspects of him too well. "This is her first calf, and she seems listless. I don't know if that's normal with Brown Swiss cows or not."

"Have you sent for the veterinarian?"

"I will if I don't see any improvement by tonight."

She looked away as she said, "I should return home. This is the day *Mamm* does the laundry and makes bread. She'll appreciate my help."

"All right." He untied the reins from the hitching post as she climbed into the buggy.

He handed her the reins, then quickly pulled back his hand. He hoped she didn't notice how the simple, chance brushing of her fingers had sent a jolt through him and left his fingers quivering. But the quick intake of her breath warned him that she had.

As he had the previous day, he stepped back and watched her drive away. Would she keep going one of these days and never come back?

Lord, he prayed, *give me the courage to ask that question before it makes me crazy. And, Lord, stand by me if she tells me she's not staying here. I'm not sure I can watch her leave another time.*

Chapter Seven

Leah could not get Esther's concerns about Ezra out of her mind. She didn't go to the Stoltzfus family's house, because she wasn't ready to speak to him again. She wanted to sort out her own baffling emotions that tugged her toward him even as *gut* sense warned her to stay away. Yet, when she looked across the fields between the farms, she noticed how he never joined his brothers tossing horseshoes at the end of the day. Was it because he was in the barn tending to his pregnant cow, or was there another reason, as Esther had suggested?

But she couldn't avoid him at the mud sale at his family's farm today. For the past week, she'd spent her spare time at *Mamm*'s treadle sewing machine, making wall hangings and crib quilts. Their *Englisch* neighbors and any tourists who might come to the auction bid wildly on any Amish quilt, no matter its size. She put the ones that were finished in a basket and walked with Mandy and *Mamm* along the road. *Daed* had decided to remain at home to finish some chores before he arrived in time for the auction.

The farm lane was edged with cars and trucks while

buggies were parked closer to the house. Timothy, Ezra's nephew, and another boy his age were unharnessing the horses and turning them out into a field. They marked the horses and the buggies with numbers so it would be simple to match them once the mud sale was over.

Mamm led the way to the back door and into the kitchen. Wanda and both her daughters were busy trying to fit into their refrigerator the extra food brought by neighbors to serve and to sell. They paused only long enough to call a greeting, then continued with their task. Other women were arranging cupcakes and cookies on plates covered with aluminum foil or making lemonade, iced tea and coffee. The large room was filled to the brim with laughter and conversation.

Leah looked around for Rose but saw no sign of Isaiah's wife. Maybe they hadn't arrived yet.

"What do you have there?" Wanda asked as she edged past some of the other women to look into Leah's basket.

"Some items for the auction."

Wanda smiled. "Those need to go out to the barn. We don't have room for anything but food in here."

"All right. Do I need to leave them with someone in particular?"

"Look for Jim Zimmermann. He's the auctioneer, and he asked that everything for the auction be brought into the barn before the bidding begins."

Leah nodded, told *Mamm* where she was going and inched her way to the door. Outside, she was glad to see Mandy playing with the other *kinder* as if she'd known them her whole life. The *kinder* swarmed over the fire truck brought from the village with squeals of excitement. While a couple of the firefighters let some of the youngsters try on the heavy coats and other pieces of their turnout gear, other *kinder* lined up for their turns. She smiled when she saw Ezra's brother, Amos, lifting off a little boy's straw hat and putting a fireman's helmet on his head. The *kind*'s smile was so big that it seemed impossible that his little face could contain it.

But tears welled up in her eyes. Johnny had loved mud sales, and he'd looked forward to the first one held in the spring. With his friends, he had sampled the different foods and watched the auction, cheering when one of the lots went for a high price. Like Ezra, he once had talked about joining the volunteer fire department. He would love today, and his absence shadowed her day.

Weaving between the buggies and through the crowd, which seemed much bigger than the population of the whole township, she went into the upper portion of the barn. It'd been swept clean, and the equipment and vehicles moved out. Hay remained stacked on one side, but chairs and a podium with a portable microphone attached had claimed the rest of the floor. People were already sitting, though the auction wasn't scheduled to begin for almost an hour.

Where was the auctioneer? She saw a thin man with hardly any hair standing on the far side of the podium. She went to him and asked if he was the auctioneer. He quickly confirmed, in his deep voice, that he was and made a place on the overflowing tables for her quilts.

Leah thanked him and started back toward the door. She halted in midstep when she saw Ezra sitting alone to one side with several empty chairs between him and the next person. He was paging through a book and didn't seem to realize she was there.

If she listened to her *gut* sense, she'd head straight back to the kitchen and help there. Even as she thought that, she went in his direction, edging along the row behind where he sat.

"That must be interesting reading," she said with a soft chuckle, putting her hands on the back of the chair beside his. "You're completely engrossed in it."

He looked up, his brown eyes as warm and welcoming as Shep's. When they twinkled at her as he smiled, she wanted to fling her arms around him and ask why they were being overly cautious about what they said to each other. Why couldn't they go back to when his easy smile had always brought one from her? No questions asked. Just best friends.

He held up the book so she could see the title on the spine. It was a book on dairy management.

"A farmer's work is never done," he said as he closed the book and set it on his lap.

"How is *Mamm Millich*?"

"She seems to be much more herself today. Doc Anstine stopped by earlier in the week and said she might simply be tired because the calf is growing quickly now. He suggested I keep her inside where she can lie down whenever she feels the need, make sure she has plenty to eat and give her a few days to get back to being herself. Looks like he's right. *Danki* for asking."

His hand slid over hers on the back of the folding chair. Not caring that there were others who could see, she put her other hand atop his. She didn't move it away as she said, "You're welcome. I'm glad she's doing better, because the plans you've made for the farm are so important to you."

"You've always seen my hopes and dreams more clearly than anyone else."

A bit of the ice around Leah's heart melted away as his words touched her. "As you've been able to see mine."

"Are your dreams the same? To be a part of this community and have *kinder* of your own?"

"I have a *kind* of my own. Mandy is my daughter, because I have raised her since the day she came home from the hospital. We—"

A man silhouetted in the door shouted Ezra's name. She moved back as Ezra stood. Instead of leaving to see why he was wanted, he gazed into her eyes. She sensed he was baffled. That she considered Mandy her own as surely as if she'd given birth to her niece? Or was it something else entirely?

"Leah, I really need to ask you about something important." His mouth tightened into a straight line when his name was called again, more urgently this time.

"Go," she urged. "We'll talk later."

"We will." He made it sound like a promise. Without another word or glance in her direction, he crossed the barn to the man who called to him.

It was Daniel, his youngest brother, she realized when she came out of the barn to see them hurrying around one side of the barn. She was curious about what was that important.

Please, God, don't let Mamm Millich *be in trouble again. Please help Ezra find his dreams.*

"Even if I'm not part of them," she whispered as she stood in the midst of the busy farmyard, feeling oddly disconnected from the scarcely controlled chaos around her.

As Leah carried a plate of whoopie pies to the table where they were being sold, she quite literally ran into

Rose Stoltzfus. She steadied the plate, then greeted Rose, who seemed to be in much better spirits.

"Leah," Rose said with a bright smile, "I'm glad you're here today. I really wanted to talk to you."

Startled, because she didn't know Rose well, she blurted as she set the plate on the table and nodded to the women selling them, "Me? Why?"

"You've known my husband since he was a little boy, and I thought we should get to know each other, too." Rose plucked at a loose thread on her apron, not meeting Leah's eyes. Every inch of her had become as taut as a fishing line with a large fish on it.

"That's a *gut* idea."

"Let's look around while we talk."

"*Ja*. I'd like that."

Almost twenty tables had been set up in the fallow field in front of the barn. Off to one side, three men tended a smoker puffing out delicious odors of meat while two grills were preparing hot dogs and hamburgers that were snapped up as soon as they finished cooking. She wasn't hungry, so she was glad when Rose turned toward the tables offering sweets and crafts and even some bedding plants.

Leah answered Rose's questions, though she found it strange that a wife wouldn't know more about her husband than Rose seemed to. Still, it was fun to relate stories from when she and Isaiah were very young scholars. She recalled some events she'd forgotten until she searched her memory for more tales of youthful adventures that always had included Johnny and Ezra, too.

She halted in the middle of a story about weeding in Wanda's garden when Rose began to cough.

"Could we move away from here?" Rose asked between coughs. "The smoke is…" She dissolved into coughing again. Her wheezing began to sound like a straining steam engine. She grabbed Leah's arm and leaned heavily on her.

"Can I do something?" Leah pulled her arm out of Rose's weakening grip and grasped her by the shoulders. "What do you need?"

Rose tried to answer but couldn't. Groping under her apron, she pulled out a small, brightly colored cylinder. She opened one end and put it in her mouth before squeezing the top.

Leah recognized the inhaler. Mandy's friend Isabella had asthma and carried one with her everywhere.

Steering Rose toward the house, she sat the younger woman on the porch steps and said she'd be right back. It took longer than usual to squeeze her way through the kitchen to get a glass of water and bring it out onto the porch, but Rose was still coughing.

She offered the glass, and Rose took it, clutching it like a lifeline. She drank, then spewed it as she continued to cough. After sucking in a second puff from her inhaler, Rose took another drink of water. Her coughing eased, but her eyes were watery as she looked up.

"*Danki*, Leah," she whispered. "I should have known better than to go over there, because I've got to be careful around smoke. It can make my throat feel like it's closing up tight."

"Can I do anything else for you? Do you want me to find Isaiah?"

She shook her head. "He's been looking forward to today. I don't want him to decide that he needs to take me home. If I'm careful to avoid the smoke, I should be okay. That bout wasn't too bad."

"Not bad?" She'd been scared as she listened to Rose trying to draw in air.

"Some of the attacks are worse."

"I'm sorry to hear that."

A hint of a smile drifted across her face. "Do you mind sitting here and chatting until my knees stop wobbling?"

"Sure." She scanned the yard and saw Mandy with *Mamm*. They were heading toward the barn to watch the auction, which must had been about to get under way. Though she wanted to go in the barn, too, she sat on the porch beside Rose.

"Tell me about Philadelphia," Rose said abruptly.

Leah glanced at her in astonishment. No one, not even *Mamm*, had asked her about the city. There had been a few questions about whether she had been happy there, but nobody was interested in the city itself.

"What would you like to know?" she asked, unsure where to begin.

"Did you live in a house there?"

She shook her head. "We had a small one-bedroom apartment. It was on the eighth story of an apartment building with forty units in total. Johnny had the bedroom."

"Where did you sleep?"

"We had two small sofas in the main room. I had one, and Mandy had the other." She could see that Rose was having a tough time imagining such a way of living.

Before she went with Johnny, Leah couldn't have envisioned living in a box like a colony of ants, either. The situation with her sleeping on the sofa was supposed to be temporary, but in the wake of Johnny's accident, moving seemed out of the question. The building had an elevator, which made his few trips beyond their door possible.

Also the doorways in the apartment were wide enough for his wheelchair.

"Oh, I had no idea."

She waited, but Rose said nothing else.

Leah decided to change the subject, "I wish I could have been here for your wedding. I'm sure it was *wunderbaar*."

"It was, and it came just in time." Rose smiled again.

"What do you mean?"

"My *mamm* wanted each of us married before we were twenty-one. I saw how miserable one of my sisters was when she wasn't married by then, so I vowed that I would not do the same. When Isaiah asked me to ride home from a singing in his courting buggy, I was already twenty. I was glad he asked me to marry him soon after that first ride together." She pressed her hands over her heart. "Oh, dear! I didn't mean that the way it sounded. I didn't accept his proposal simply to marry before I was twenty-one. I was in love with him." Color rushed her face. "I *am* in love with him."

It was such a blessing to see Rose Stoltzfus happy. Isaiah's wife was truly pretty when her face wasn't puffy from tears.

"Wanda told me," Rose went on, "that you made those beautiful quilts that Amos has at his store. Did you do them by hand?"

"Most of the piecing I did on a sewing machine, but I always quilt the layers together by hand. Do you like to sew?"

"*Ja*. Isaiah says he will buy me a sewing machine after he finishes that big project he is doing for the new restaurant down the road from the Stoltzfus Family Shops. They have ordered railings to use as half walls and iron beams, and even a circular staircase to lead up to what will be an outdoors dining room on the roof. He has been working on the pieces for weeks." Her smile faltered. "Working for very long hours, because the projects must be completed and installed in order for the restaurant to open."

"What a *gut* husband he is to work that hard in order to provide for you and get you the sewing machine you want! You were wise to accept his proposal. The Stoltzfus brothers are hardworking and want to provide for their families as their *daed* did."

"Isaiah is a *gut* husband, isn't he?" Her eyes refilled with tears. "I pray I can be the wife he deserves. And the *Leit* deserves, though I don't know if I can ever do that."

"No one expects you to be perfect, least of all God. He knows that, no matter how hard we try, perfection is only a goal, not something we can ever attain. It's that we try…that is what matters."

"You should be the new minister's wife. You know the right things to say. Of course, you'd need to be a wife before you could be a minister's wife." Rose looked at her squarely. "Everyone says that you and Ezra spent a lot of time together before you left. Why didn't you get married?"

Leah knew she was blushing, because her face felt as if it'd burst into flame. "We were *gut* friends. That's all."

"He's unwed, and so are you." Coming to her feet, Rose patted Leah's shoulder. "That's something you should keep in mind."

Glad that Rose walked away without expecting an answer, Leah wondered what the younger woman would have said if Leah had spoken the truth that Ezra was seldom far from her thoughts. She stared at the barn. Ezra must be inside now that the auction had started. Had he heard the two of them were the topic of gossip?

She got up and went into the house. The kitchen was deserted, and she whispered a prayer of thanks that she was able to be alone. She couldn't hide forever, but she wasn't ready to chance seeing Ezra until she had her emotions under better control.

Ezra looked up as a shadow crossed over where he sat at one end of a row of chairs. His hope that Leah had returned was dampened when he saw Isaiah drop onto the empty chair next to him.

"You're not saving this for someone, are you?" his brother asked.

"No."

"Gut." He glanced toward the podium where Jim Zimmermann held up a basket filled with honey from the Millers' farm. "I thought you might be saving it for Leah."

He didn't rise to his brother's bait, saying only, "As far as I know, she's busy helping *Mamm* and the other women."

"That sounds like Leah."

"Ja. She wants to help everyone." He hoped Isaiah didn't hear the tinge of bitterness in his voice.

"Maybe she can help Rose." His brother combed his fingers back through his hair. "I knew Rose wouldn't be happy if I was selected by the lot, but every time I've come into the house this week, I can see that she's been crying. She is upset that she's now a minister's wife. Maybe if Leah spends some time with her, Rose can stop thinking about her unhappiness and start to be happy

again. Leah has always been such a cheerful person."
He hesitated, then asked, "Is she still?"

"From what I can see, she's trying to be."

"That's *gut* enough for me. Will you ask her to come
over and see Rose?"

"Why don't you? You've been friends with her as long
as I have."

"I don't want Rose to find out that I was involved."

Ezra grimaced. "Why not? Wouldn't she appreciate
you caring about her enough to ask Leah to stop by?"

"Normally I'd say yes, but now…"

Seeing the despair on his brother's face, Ezra relented.
Poor Isaiah didn't know which way to jump, because everything he did seemed to add to Rose's distress. Could
Leah make a difference? He wasn't sure, but he knew
she'd do her best. She never did anything less. Perhaps
her faith that God was with her through *gut* times and
bad would help Rose believe the same.

Even though I question that myself. He hated the way
his conscience spoke up like that. He'd always considered his faith strong enough to handle anything. The
past decade had been challenging in more ways than he
could count. He had tried to cling to his belief that God
walked beside him, holding him up when life beat him
down, but after Leah vanished, he'd begun questioning
every part of his life.

"All right," he said. "I'll ask Leah to go and see Rose
when she can."

"*Danki*, big brother." Isaiah's face lightened like the
sun breaking through storm clouds. "Isn't that Leah's
work?"

Ezra nodded as he looked at the colorful, small quilts
Leah had been carrying when she came into the barn

earlier. He knew that she thought he'd been absorbed in his reading and hadn't seen her until she stopped behind his chair. It was impossible to be unaware of her. Even though her buoyant spirit had become heavy during her time away, a joyous glow about her refused to be dimmed.

He had a tough time paying attention to the auction after Leah's quilts were sold because his thoughts bounced back to Leah any time he tried to think of something else. By the time the auction was over, he hadn't bid on the seeder he'd hoped to buy. He didn't know who bought it or for how much. While his brother chatted with the men sitting around them, Ezra skirted the group and headed out of the barn.

His gaze settled on Leah instantly as if a sign glowed above her head. She stood on the porch and was looking up at the sky. A raindrop struck his nose as he strode across the yard. Behind him, people called out to each other as they grabbed items off the table and rushed into the barn to keep them dry. He was surprised when Leah didn't rush to help, but then he realized that she'd seen him coming toward her.

"Wie bischt?" he asked as he came up the steps to stand beside her. "How are you doing?"

She smiled. "You don't have to translate everything into English. I may have lived away for a long time, but I haven't forgotten my first language."

"You're right." He watched as the sprinkle changed into a downpour. "I guess I'm uncertain because I don't want to offend you."

"Offend me? How?"

"I can't imagine how you lived in that big city, and I don't want to. But I do know ten years is a very long time. I'm not certain what you've forgotten or what habits you learned from *Englischers*, and I don't want to make you uncomfortable. Especially in front of others."

Her smile softened, and his heart did a twirl in his chest. It seemed to spin even faster when she said, "Ezra, I'm glad to discover that, in spite of everything, one thing hasn't changed. You're still a *gut* friend to me."

He looked hastily away as his heart thudded down into his gut. Friend? Was that how she thought of him? Was that how she had always thought of him? Maybe wanting them to become something more had been only his wish.

His thoughts made his voice gruff as he said, "Isaiah asked if I would ask you to do him a favor."

"Why doesn't he ask me himself?"

"He didn't want Rose to see you two talking together. He thought that might make Rose more upset."

"I can understand that. What's this favor he wants me to do?"

"He'd like you to spend time with Rose. He hopes you can become friends, and that your friendship will help her through this difficult time."

She rolled her eyes, looking as annoyed as her niece could. "You're too late. Rose and I have already begun to get to know one another. There's no need to concoct some great scheme in the shadows."

"Isaiah is very worried about her."

"I know." She looked back out at the rain as she added, "Rose asked me about Philadelphia. She had a lot of questions. You don't think that she's considering leaving Paradise Springs, do you?"

He leaned against the pole that held up the porch roof. "You're asking the wrong man, Leah. No one was more surprised than I was when *you* left Paradise Springs."

"I was pretty surprised myself."

His lips twitched in a reluctant smile. "Knowing what I do now, I'm sure you were." He became serious again as he said, "Esther told me how you spent time with Mandy at school several days this week. You are very protective of your niece."

"Go ahead. You can say it. I'm overprotective."

"That's not for me to judge. I can't help wondering if there's another reason you're worried. Do you fear Mandy's *mamm* will come here to claim her?"

"No."

He gave her a moment to add something more, and when she didn't, he said, "You sound very definite."

"*Ja*, I am. As I told you before, Mandy's *mamm*, Carleen, disappeared within days after Johnny's accident, even though Mandy was only a few weeks old. I contacted some of Carleen's friends to discover where she'd gone."

"Did you find her?"

"Not exactly. She must have learned I was looking for her, because she left a message with one of those friends to tell me to stop looking for her, that she didn't want anything more to do with either Johnny or their daughter or settling down in one place. A couple of months later, a letter arrived from a lawyer's office in Colorado. It was a form to relinquish any claim on Mandy so Johnny could let someone else adopt her if he wanted. Instead, he had me named as her legal guardian."

"I had no idea."

"It's not something we talk about. I don't want Mandy being reminded that her birth *mamm* abandoned her."

Now it was his turn to be silent. He tried to imagine someone in their community giving up their *kind* simply because it was an inconvenience. Even if a member of the

Leit couldn't care for a *kind*, someone within the district would take that little one into their home and rear it as their own. Each *boppli* was a blessing from God, a way to remind them that love was His greatest gift.

He watched her, wondering if now was the time to ask if *she* were staying or leaving again. Maybe it was, but he didn't want to destroy the camaraderie they shared as they watched the rain. He yearned for more than friendship with her, but he was glad for this quiet moment when they could be content in each other's company.

Leah tried to match her steps to Ezra's longer strides as they walked side by side under an umbrella along the road between his house and hers. No cars or trucks rushed past. She dodged a couple of big puddles that were pocked with more rain. The umbrella was large, but her shoulder pressed against his arm on every step. She could have moved farther away, but that meant being out in the rain.

And, to be honest, she relished being close to him. The casual brush of his shoulder against hers sent a lightning-quick pulse through her. He was silent, and that was fine. She appreciated the feeling of the company of someone who didn't try to act as if she were some sort of weird creature because she'd gone away, and, more important, he understood how she was struggling to help Mandy—and herself—fit into the community.

"Here we are," she said when they paused at the end of the lane that led to her family's farm. Rain slapped the broad leaves on the trees and made the grass dance as the rain fell in a soft patter.

When she started to ease out from beneath the umbrella, Ezra said, "You keep it."

Warmth suffused her throat as Mari offered a stiff nod and a hasty "Good morning," before turning her attention to her unfinished breakfast. Mari didn't want anyone to get the idea that she'd come to Seven Poplars so Sara could find her a husband. That was the last thing on her mind.

"Going to be working for Gideon and Addy, I hear," James remarked as he added milk to his coffee from a small pitcher on the table.

Mari slowly lifted her gaze. James had nice hands. She raised her eyes higher to find that he was still watching her intently, but it wasn't a predatory gaze. James seemed genuinely friendly rather than coming on to her, as if he was interested in what she had to say. "I hope so." She suddenly felt shy, and she had no idea why. "I don't know a thing about butcher shops."

"You'll pick it up quick." James took a sip of his coffee. "And Gideon is a great guy. He'll make it fun. Don't you think so, Sara?"

Sara looked from James to Mari and then back at James. "I agree." She smiled and took a sip of her coffee. "I think Mari's a fine candidate for all sorts of things."

Don't miss
A HUSBAND FOR MARI
by Emma Miller,
available February 2016 wherever
Love Inspired® books and ebooks are sold.

SPECIAL EXCERPT FROM

Love Inspired

As a young woman seeks a better life for herself
and her son in Amish country, will she find happiness
and love with an Amish carpenter?

Read on for a sneak preview of
A HUSBAND FOR MARI,
the second book in the new series
THE AMISH MATCHMAKER.

"That's James," Sara the matchmaker explained in
English. "He's the one charging me an outrageous amount
for the addition to my house."

"You want craftsmanship, you have to pay for it,"
James answered confidently. He strode into the kitchen,
opened a cupboard, removed a coffee mug and poured
himself a cup. "We're the best, and you wouldn't be
satisfied with anyone else."

He glanced at Mari. "This must be your new
houseguest. Mari, is it?"

"*Ya*, this is my friend Mari." Sara introduced her. "She
and her son, Zachary, will be here with me for a while, so
I expect you to make her feel welcome."

"Pleased to meet you, Mari," James said. The foreman's
voice was pleasant, his penetrating eyes strikingly
memorable. Mari felt a strange ripple of exhilaration as
James's strong face softened into a genuine smile, and he
held her gaze for just a fraction of a second longer than
was appropriate.

"It's not raining that hard. I can run to the house."

"*Ja*, but keep the umbrella." He tugged on one of her *kapp* strings as he did to tease her years ago. "I'm used to getting wet out in these fields."

"So am I."

"True." He winked at her as she took the umbrella, making sure she held it high enough so he didn't have to stoop. "There was the time you met me with the garden hose because you were mad at me for not sharing *Mamm*'s peanut butter cookies and ended up almost as wet as me."

"They were *chocolate* peanut butter cookies! The best cookies in the world. Don't tell my *mamm* I said that."

"As long as you don't tell mine that no one makes better corn chowder than your *mamm*."

"A deal." She held out her hand, grinning.

Her smile softened as he took her hand in both of his. She gazed into his eyes, which were shadowed by the murky day. Gently he squeezed her fingers before he slowly released them. He lightly brushed a recalcitrant strand of her hair back toward her *kapp*, and a frisson inched down her back as that cold around her heart eased further.

There were so many things she wanted to say, but the moment passed when a car came around the corner. They moved off the road, and the driver kindly slowed down so they weren't splashed by water coming off the tires. The man waved before the car went beyond the next hill.

Ezra must have realized it was the wrong time to speak, too, because he left then and hurried home through the rain. She watched him until he vanished around the corner before she headed along the lane. Her steps were as light as if she bounced on clouds instead of the gravel lane. In rhythm with the rain falling on the umbrella, she

hummed a tuneless song. Her happiness was simply too powerful to keep inside her.

She knew that as soon as she reached the house *Mamm* and Mandy would want to talk about the mud sale. This was her only time to savor the wonder left by Ezra's touch. He had not pushed the boundaries of friendship; still, she longed to believe the warmth in his eyes heralded that he wanted more. Could they pick up where they had left off ten years ago when they had been hardly old enough to consider courting? The thought was both thrilling and terrifying because they weren't the same people they'd been back then.

The lane curved between the main barn and the house. As she strolled toward the house, *Daed* came out of the barn. She heard Mandy's shout seconds before the little girl appeared in the barn's doorway. Her *daed* turned and tumbled to the ground. He was still except for his right hand, which struggled to grasp the grass. He raised his head, then collapsed with a groan.

Chapter Eight

Leah wasn't surprised when, as she and *Mamm* assisted *Daed* toward the house, he refused to let them call 911, but she was astonished that *Mamm* agreed. With an expression that warned Leah not to argue, *Mamm* kept an arm around him as she warned him of a stone or a bush in their way. Leah ran ahead to the kitchen door. As she held it open, she glanced at Mandy, who stood by the pump with Shep in her arms. The little girl's face was as colorless as her apron.

She longed to comfort Mandy, but she went with *Mamm* to help her get *Daed* to his favorite chair in the living room. He sat heavily with a groan and leaned his head back against it. She swept the quilt off the back of the sofa. When she started to place it over him, he put up his hands.

"I'm not an invalid," he ordered. "Don't treat me like one."

"You need to see a doctor. You fell again," Leah said as she tucked the quilt around him in spite of his words.

He glowered at her. "I stumbled. I need to have Mandy

mow the grass tomorrow, because it's gotten too long and is as slippery as ice when it's wet."

Mandy came in and said nothing as she waited in the doorway between the kitchen and front room. She held Shep close until the dog wiggled to get down.

Shep ran over to Leah and sat by her side. She looked from the dog to Mandy, whose face became even more colorless if possible.

"Will you get *Grossdawdi* a cup of coffee?" *Mamm* asked the little girl.

"Ja." She spun on her heel and rushed back into the kitchen.

By the time Mandy had returned, carefully balancing the cup of black coffee, *Daed* was seated with his feet up on a small stool and a pillow behind his head. He wouldn't even talk about lying down and resting, but Leah could see he was unnerved by the way his hands shook when he reached for the cup.

Mandy set it on a table beside the chair, then scurried toward the front door, pausing only long enough to shoot a glance at Leah. Seeing her niece's drawn face, Leah gave her a steadying smile before following *Mamm* into the kitchen.

Her *mamm* went to the stove and turned the burner on under the stew pot. She began to stir it, releasing the scent of beef and vegetables.

Leah put her hand on the counter by the sink and asked in a low voice that wouldn't reach *Daed* in the other room, "How long has this been happening?"

"Your *daed* being clumsy?" She stirred the stew vigorously. "Every day of his life."

"*Mamm*, what happened wasn't him being clumsy. There wasn't anything for him to stumble over."

"He said he slipped on the wet grass."

"And you believe him?"

"He's my husband." She didn't look at Leah. "Why wouldn't I believe him?"

Leah tried to calm her voice, but it rose on each word she spoke. "Because he isn't being honest, *Mamm*. I don't know if it's because he doesn't want to worry you or he's frightened, but he should see a doctor. It might be nothing more than a simple ear infection. Those can make someone very dizzy."

"Let me tend to him, Leah." She turned from the stove and patted Leah's cheek gently. "Your concern shows your love for your *daed*, but you've become too accustomed to *Englisch* ways. I will check his ears tonight. If I see any sign of redness, I'll flush them with peroxide."

"And if you don't see any signs of redness?"

Mamm shrugged and didn't answer.

The frustration she'd endured while listening to *Daed* and Johnny quarrel came rushing back. She clenched her hands to keep from throwing them up in irritation. If her *daed* and brother had—just once—faced the fact they might have some common ground, they could have patched up their differences. Every time she'd suggested that, they'd refused to listen.

Now *Mamm* was doing the same. Ignoring the facts was wrong. Helping *Daed* was the right thing to do. For a second, she considered contacting the village clinic for advice, but God's commandment urged her to honor her parents. Obeying had never been so hard.

"Leah?" *Mamm* turned from the stove and wiped her hands on a dish towel.

"Ja?"

"Your *daed* is, despite his efforts not to be, a proud

man. Don't say anything to anyone else about this and caution Mandy to say nothing, too."

"I will agree if you will agree that if this happens again, we'll call the clinic in the village."

"I can't agree. The decision isn't mine."

Leah nodded, accepting defeat. She mumbled something about checking on Mandy. Pouring three glasses of lemonade, she set one on the counter by her *mamm* and picked up the other two. She glanced at *Daed* as she tiptoed through the front room. He was leaning his head back, with his eyes closed. His face was flushed, and he tapped the arm in the chair. If she hadn't seen him fall, she would never have guessed anything was amiss. Was she making something out of what was truly nothing?

God, I need Your guidance to help Daed. *Please guide me in the right direction.* She repeated the prayer over and over silently as she crossed the room and went out the front door, closing it behind her.

As she'd expected, Mandy sat on one of the pair of rocking chairs on the porch. Shep was curled up on her lap. He looked up and wagged his tail when Leah crossed the porch. Beyond the roof, the rain fell, watering the freshly planted fields that stretched into the twilight. Several cars whooshed past out on the road, their lights flickering as they pierced the storm.

It seemed impossible that less than an hour ago, she had been standing out there with Ezra, happier than she'd been in a long time. Now she felt confused and thwarted at every turn.

She handed Mandy a glass before sitting on the other rocker. With a sigh, she tried to smile at the little girl and failed. She couldn't pretend nothing was wrong.

"How is *Grossdawdi*, Aunt Leah?" The little girl trembled almost as much as *Daed* had. "Is he going to die?"

"No, not now." She hoped she was being honest. "*Grossmammi* is going to check if he has an ear infection. That could have made him dizzy enough to trip."

Mandy shook her head vehemently as she continued to pet Shep. "It wasn't an ear infection that made him to fall down." She took a drink as she petted Shep. "He showed me what really was going on."

"I only saw him fall. What did you see before that? Was he unsteady when he was walking in the barn? Did he—"

"I'm not talking about *Grossdawdi* Abram. I meant Shep."

"What about him?"

"He did his special dance just before *Grossdawdi* fell down."

Leah swallowed her gasp as she squeaked out, "The same one he did when your *daed* was about to have a seizure?"

She nodded, her eyes wide with fear. "What do you think it means?"

"I'm not sure." Was that the truth, or was she, like *Mamm*, trying to act as if nothing were wrong with *Daed*?

She struggled to recall every tiny detail she'd been told by the people who'd trained Shep as a service dog. Before he had come to live in the apartment with them, he'd learned how to discern the changes that occurred in the human brain before a seizure was about to begin. Those lessons had been ingrained in him months before he met Johnny for the first time. It hadn't taken him long to recognize the unique smells he could pick up before one of Johnny's seizures began. Maybe a couple of weeks.

Shep had been on the farm about the same amount of time before *Daed* fell and bumped his head in the kitchen on Mandy's first day of school. That day, while *Mamm* bandaged *Daed*, Shep went through the motions he had been taught to perform in the wake of his warning about an upcoming seizure.

Was it possible that *Daed* had suffered something similar and that was why he fell? He hadn't acted as confused as Johnny had after a seizure, and he had seemed to be in control of his limbs. What had Shep sensed? She couldn't believe it was a coincidence. Not when it had happened twice now.

She glanced at the front door but knew she couldn't blurt out her suspicions to *Mamm*. Mandy was telling the truth…of what she thought she'd seen. Shep did have a unique way of leaping about on his hind feet when Johnny had been about to have a seizure, but the little dog was easily excitable and often jumped. Mandy had been watching from the barn, and *Daed* had been halfway to the house. From that distance, it would be difficult to see exactly what Shep was doing.

"Mandy, if Shep starts doing that dance again, I want you to scream as loud as you can for *Mamm* or me. Maybe Shep is sensing something about *Daed* losing his balance. If one of us can get there fast enough, we might be able to prevent him from falling and hurting himself again."

"I can—"

Leah shook her head as she took Mandy's hand in hers. "He is too big for you to hold up on your own. That's why I want you to scream at the top of your lungs. Two of us together should be able to keep him on his feet." Looking into her niece's eyes, she ached when she saw her twin brother in Mandy's expression. "You spend a lot of time

with your *grossdawdi* as he's working around the farm. Can we depend on you to call us?"

"*Ja!* Me and Shep will guard *Grossdawdi*." Her thin chest puffed out with determination to do as she promised. It deflated as quickly when she asked, "But what about when I'm in school?"

"*Mamm* and I will keep an eye on him then."

"School will be done in a few weeks. After that, Shep and I are going to stick like glue to *Grossdawdi*."

Knowing her niece needed time to be a *kind*, Leah smiled. "Once you're out of school, we'll arrange a schedule that works for all of us." She reached to tug Mandy's *kapp* string, then paused as she remembered Ezra doing that to hers.

A high-pitched howl rang through the deepening darkness, followed by staccato yelps. Shep jumped to his feet on Mandy's lap, his head snapping in the direction of the sounds.

"What's that?" cried Mandy.

Shep whined deep in his throat, his hair rising around his collar as the sound came again.

"A coyote or a coydog, I'd guess." Leah shuddered. "Let's go inside." She didn't want to add that either a coyote or its mixed offspring could easily kill a small dog like Shep.

"I don't like that sound," Mandy said, not moving. "We didn't hear anything like that in Philadelphia."

Though coyotes likely roamed the city, Leah didn't correct the little girl.

"I miss home." Mandy got to her feet and held Shep close. Pausing in front of Leah, she asked, "How much longer are we staying here? Isabella's tenth birthday is only a few weeks from now, and I don't want to miss her

party. I should be getting my invitation soon, but she told me that it's going to be a sleepover. I can go, can't I? I can't wait. My very first sleepover."

Fortunately Mandy didn't wait for an answer as she hurried into the house, chattering about the party.

Leah sank back into the rocking chair. She ignored the coyotes' calls as she stared out into the rain. Facing the truth wasn't easy, but though Mandy might wear plain clothes and follow the *Ordnung* of their district, to the little girl, it was only a game. She hadn't given up her longing to return to the city and the life and friends and dreams she had there.

If they returned to Philadelphia, Leah would have to leave everything behind again...including her reblooming relationship with Ezra. Yet, she couldn't put her happiness ahead of Mandy's. She had to find a way to show Mandy that their lives in Paradise Springs were better than in the city, but how? She pressed her hands together and closed her eyes. "God, show me the way because I don't have any idea what to do."

She hoped God would send her inspiration soon.

Ezra drew in the reins to slow his buggy when he saw Leah standing by the mailbox at the end of the Beilers' lane early the next week. Dozens of emotions rushed through him, but the only one he paid attention to was his anticipation to enjoy another conversation with her. Maybe he'd even have the opportunity to hold her slender fingers again.

Not looking in his direction, she closed the mailbox and glanced at the handful of envelopes she had taken out. A frown furrowed a line between her brows. Was she

disappointed that a letter hadn't arrived from someone special? From a suitor she'd left behind in Philadelphia?

When he imagined some *Englischer* writing to her or perhaps some Amish man she'd encountered at the market in the city, an odd sensation pinched him. A sensation he didn't want to examine too closely. *Are you envious of someone who may not even exist?* He ignored the taunting voice in his head.

The horse rattled the harness, and she looked up. Strain had stolen the usual glow from her face. "*Wie bischt*, Ezra?"

As he answered that he was doing fine, he admitted to himself that he liked hearing her use plain words. It was as if each word washed away some of the *Englisch* influence that had seeped into her life. He wanted to believe that meant she had no thoughts of leaving again.

"Bad news?" he asked when she scowled at the envelopes she held.

"Not exactly." She pulled out a small, bright pink envelope. "Mandy has been waiting for this impatiently. It's an invitation to her best friend Isabella's birthday party."

"In Philadelphia?" He struggled to get the words out, feeling as if someone had punched him in the gut.

She slid the envelope back in among the others. *"Ja."*

"Are you going to give it to her?"

"Ja. I won't be dishonest with her." She sighed. "I don't know what will happen now. I've been praying for guidance."

"I'll add my prayers to yours, Leah."

Her face brightened, and she reached out to clasp his sleeve. "*Danki*, Ezra. I know God listens to each of our prayers, so it can't hurt to have more going up."

Savoring the tingle that flew up his arm, he started to

move his hand to put it over hers. She drew her fingers
back and held the envelopes with both hands. He couldn't
be sure if she'd seen his motion and reacted to it or not.
As unsettled as she was by the invitation addressed to
Mandy, he didn't want to upset her further.

Instead, he said, "I thought you'd want to know that
we raised almost four thousand dollars at the mud sale."

"That's *wunderbaar!*"

"Jim the auctioneer told me that your quilts sold for
over one hundred dollars each."

"Really?" Her eyes widened in honest shock. "For
such small pieces?"

"I recognized a couple of the bidders. One has a shop
in Bird-in-Hand and the other has one in Strasburg. I'm
sure they plan to resell the small quilts to tourists for
even more than that."

"Where are you going?"

"Into town. I'm hoping Joshua can fix a wheel that
broke on my hay wagon." He pointed to the cargo space
behind the buggy's cab that made the vehicle resemble
an *Englischer*'s pickup truck. A large wheel balanced in
the open bed.

"Will you let Amos know that I'll come in tomorrow
and pick up the groceries *Mamm* ordered? We were supposed to pick them up today, but Mandy is staying late at
school today to work on a project. She won't be home for
another hour, and…" She looked down at the envelopes.

Was she hiding more than distress about Mandy being
invited to her friend's party? "I'd be glad to give you a
ride if you want to get them today."

Her smile was brittle, and her eyes shifted away as
if she suddenly found the dandelions by the road very
interesting. "No, but *danki*. I've got some chores I need

to finish. I didn't want Amos to stay late at the store because he expects me to come today. If you don't mind telling him…"

Before he could say that he did mind because he was growing surer with every word she spoke that there was something very important that she wasn't telling him, she hurried back toward the house. She ran so fast that the strings on her heart-shaped *kapp* bounced out behind her.

Ezra rested his elbows on his knees as he watched her disappear around the barn, then he slapped the reins gently against the horse. The buggy rolled along the side of the road, and the questions followed, taunting him. When he'd walked with Leah after the mud sale, he had believed that she was opening up to him as she'd done years ago. Now she was as closed as a miser's fist.

As if the weather had grown as dejected as he was, rain spit against the windshield. He leaned forward and flipped the switches to turn on the buggy's lights. The trees along the road were becoming obscured in mist, and he wanted to be as visible as possible to any other traffic.

Only a few cars were parked in the parking lot in front of the Stoltzfus Family Shops. They were closer to Amos's grocery store than Joshua's buggy shop. The carpentry shop where his youngest brothers worked was dark, so they must be working on a project somewhere in the area.

Lashing the reins to the hitching post, Ezra wrestled the broken wheel out of the back of the buggy. He carried it into the shop and leaned it against the high counter at the front of the shop. Both his brother and his nephew Timothy paused in their work around the buggies and glanced toward the door.

"Can you fix this?" Ezra asked in lieu of a greeting.

Joshua stood from where he had been kneeling beside a family buggy that looked finished except for paint. Wiping his hands on a stained cloth, he came over to examine the wheel. He ran his finger expertly along the area where the metal rim had separated from the wooden one.

"Ja," he said, "but it may take a few days. I don't know if I have the right length of metal to put around a wheel this size."

"Can't you hammer this back into place? I need it to finish cutting the hay in the big field." He glanced at the window. "Once it stops raining long enough."

"Not if you don't want to be back here tomorrow with it broken again. Cobbling it together won't do you any *gut*. The first time it hits a stone or even a small hill in the field, it may break again."

"Do you have a wheel here that I can use until you can fix this one? I've lost enough time to the rain as it is. I don't know why God sends us too much rain some years and not enough others."

"To teach us faith that things will eventually work out for the best."

Ezra laughed tautly, a short, sharp sound that brought a frown from his brother. "Do you have a wheel I can use or not?"

"I'll look, but not until you tell me what's wrong with you. You're as grumpy as a beaver with a toothache."

Timothy chuckled. He swept the sawdust with more enthusiasm when his *daed* frowned in his direction.

"Sorry," Ezra said. "I got frustrated over something, and you shouldn't have to suffer because of it."

"Leah?"

"Is it that obvious?" He grimaced. "It must be."

"You two seemed to be getting along well at the mud sale."

"I thought so, but, today when I offered her a ride here to pick up her family's groceries, it was as if she couldn't wait to get away from me."

"Why?"

"I don't know."

Joshua frowned. "Didn't you ask her?"

"No. I didn't want to be nosy."

"But isn't that better than you imagining all sorts of reasons—none of which may have any basis in reality— why she didn't accept your offer?" He hooked a thumb toward Timothy, who was dumping the sawdust into a barrel at the back of the shop. "I would expect such foolishness from him, but not from a full-grown man."

Ezra arched his brows and shook his head. "Maybe that's the problem. When I'm around her, I find myself thinking like a teenager again. As if no time has passed since the night she and Johnny went away."

"Ten years have gone by, Ezra." He sighed. "Ten years of happiness and sorrow and changes. Even if you wished to, you can't erase them and pretend they haven't happened."

"I don't intend to try, but..." He wasn't sure what the "but" would be. He knew there had to be one. Otherwise, why was he miserable?

"When I find myself struggling with wishing that the past was different, I remind myself of the words in Psalm 118."

Ezra knew the verse his brother was referring to, because he had often heard Joshua murmur the words to himself in the days, weeks and months after his beloved Matilda had died.

*This is the day which the Lord hath made; we will re-
joice and be glad in it.*

"Those words got me through many lonely days and
nights," Joshua continued when Ezra remained silent. "I'd
become accustomed to sharing dreams of the future with
Matilda, but suddenly she was gone. The past was too
painful, and the future was an empty landscape. All I had
was the present. I needed to be the *daed* for our *kinder*
that she would have wanted me to be. All you have is the
present, too, Ezra. That you can change. Not the past."

"Danki." Ezra patted his brother on the arm, hoping
that the motion would say what words couldn't.

But Joshua wasn't done. "You've got a great opportunity. I don't see any reason why the two of you can't
start over, if that's what you want."

"Maybe we could, if we wanted to."

Joshua snorted his disbelief. "Wanted to? You can't
stop talking about her, and you're worrying yourself sick
over silly things."

"What if she leaves again?" Ezra asked, finally voic-
ing his greatest fear.

"Is she planning to?" His brother looked astonished.
"From what *Mamm* and Esther have told me, she seems
really happy to be home."

"She is, but her niece isn't." He explained the little
he knew about the birthday party invitation. "You know
Leah. She puts her needs and wants aside if someone
needs her help. If Mandy is adamant about going back to
Philadelphia, do you think Leah will let her go alone?"

"No." Joshua scratched behind his ear. "But the solu-
tion is easy."

"Really?"

"You need to make sure Mandy wants to stay here.

If she doesn't go, Leah won't. Look, I can ask Rose if Mandy can come over and play with Deborah."

"Rose is babysitting for you?"

"She agreed to watch Levi and Deborah after school. I lost my regular sitter Betty last week after she took a job cleaning Walt Filipowski's bed-and-breakfast over on Meadow Lane." Leaning an elbow on the counter, he said, "If Mandy is happy with new friends, she'll find it easier to let the old ones go."

Ezra considered his brother's suggestions. They were simple and straightforward and would truly benefit Mandy because she could make a home in Paradise Springs. Maybe even be baptized into their faith eventually and truly become a part of the *Leit*.

"You can do that," Joshua added, "or you could ask Leah if she intends to return to the city with Mandy."

"I can't."

"Why not?" His brother frowned. "It's a simple enough question—are you staying or going back to Philadelphia?"

"If I back her into a corner, she might decide then and there that she's not staying. I don't want to be the cause of her leaving a second time."

"A second time? She left last time because of Johnny, right?"

"I hope so." He went out of the shop before Joshua could ask another question, but he couldn't escape the truth he'd tried to ignore from the moment he'd first heard that Leah had left Paradise Springs with her brother.

What if she'd gone away because of the kiss he'd stolen from her? He'd been tongue-tied afterward, overwhelmed by his feelings for her. He hadn't been able to think of anything to say. He'd gotten up and left. He didn't even

walk her home. The next day, he'd watched for a chance to go and talk with her alone, but her twin brother or one of her parents was with her throughout the day.

Then she was gone.

Since then, he'd wondered if he'd backed her into a corner, kissing her and leaving without a word as if the kiss meant nothing. As if *she* meant nothing.

He couldn't risk making the same mistake, but asking her to choose between Mandy and him would be an even bigger error. There must be some way to keep both her and Mandy in Paradise Springs. But how?

Chapter Nine

Where could Mandy be? *Mamm* hadn't seen her for the past hour, though she knew Mandy had come home from school, because she'd made a batch of oatmeal raisin cookies with her granddaughter.

Leah found no sign of the girl or Shep in any of the outbuildings. She saw *Daed* working out behind the barn. He was repairing the belt on the stationary engine that ran some of the equipment on the farm. For once, Mandy wasn't near where he was.

Where else could she be on a Saturday?

Shadowing her eyes, Leah looked across the field toward Ezra's farm. The milk herd was scattered in one field as the cows grazed. Clothes hung on the line stretching from the house to the barn, but no one was in the yard. She looked along the fence lines that she could see from where she stood, but Mandy wasn't in sight.

She opened the gate on her family's side of the field. She picked her way across the field as quickly as she could. She didn't want to leave *Mamm* home without someone else there very long. Just in case *Daed* fell again. That was why she'd turned down Ezra's offer to

drive her to the grocery store to pick up *Mamm*'s order. The next day, when Mandy was home from school, Leah had collected the groceries knowing that her niece would help, if necessary. She thanked God again that it hadn't been.

The days of rain had left the ground muddy, and pockets of water were hidden beneath the thick grass. When her foot sank into one, she grimaced and focused on watching where she walked. She made it across the field without soaking her other sneaker.

She understood why the house had appeared deserted when she saw that the family's buggy was gone. Wanda and Esther must be calling on someone or running errands. Was Ezra gone, too? She didn't see anyone working in any of the fields, which was odd for him on a Saturday. With all the rain, he'd been out cutting hay whenever the skies were clear.

A sharp bark caught Leah's ear. Looking at the field behind the barn, the one she hadn't been able to view from home, she saw Mandy. The little girl was leaning over the fence, her bare toes curled on top of the lowest rail and holding her hand out toward some cows, who regarded her with indifference. Shep had his head stuck through the railing and seemed to believe that the cows understood what his barking meant.

"Mandy!" she said as she hurried to where her niece stood. "You know you're supposed to let someone know when you're leaving the farm."

Glancing over her shoulder with a smile, her niece waved the handful of grass toward the cows, but they had no interest in being fed that way. "I can't see where *Mamm Millich* is. Do you see her? Do you think she's

had her calf? I want to be able to get a photo of the calf to show Isabella when I go to her party."

"Mandy, you need to check with someone before you go running off," she said. So far, Mandy hadn't said anything about the birthday party in front of her grandparents, as Leah had asked. The little girl hadn't asked why, and Leah suspected she understood it would be a sore point with *Mamm* and *Daed*. Now wasn't the time to discuss either taking pictures or the birthday party. "*Mamm* and I have been worried sick when we couldn't find you."

That finally got Mandy's attention. She let the grass fall to the ground and jumped down off the fence, her dark skirt swirling around her knees. "I told *Grossdawdi* that I was going to come over here to see my favorite cow." The little girl regarded her, baffled. "Didn't he tell you?"

"He was busy, so I didn't ask him if he knew where you were." She wasn't going to admit that she wasn't sure if she would have asked her *daed* about Mandy's whereabouts even if he hadn't been involved in fixing the engine belt.

In large part that was because she hadn't wanted to worry him. She was unsure if his heart was the reason he kept falling, but she knew that worry wasn't *gut* for someone with heart disease. She hadn't had much time to observe him to see if she could discern what really was causing him to lose his footing and fall. He'd spent most of his time out in the barn or in the fields. The only time he came inside was for meals and for evening devotionals before bed. It was as if he were trying to crowd a year's work into a month. Did he, even though he argued otherwise, think that he was seriously ill? She wished he would heed her when she pleaded with him to see a doctor.

Would he listen to another man? Someone like the bishop or the deacon maybe. Suggesting that might make him even more determined to conceal his illness because he didn't want to be a financial burden on the *Leit*.

Exactly like the excuse Johnny had used not to come home.

Daed was too much like his only son, stubborn and sure that he was right even in the face of facts that showed otherwise. She hoped he wouldn't kill himself trying to disprove the truth that he needed medical help.

She sighed, knowing she was being exactly as stubborn. She should have gone to speak with *Daed* and asked if he knew where Mandy was. No matter where *Daed* went when Mandy wasn't at school, she followed him around, asking questions, and offering to help with chores. Leah guessed it was her way of keeping an eye on her *grossdawdi* because Shep always joined her, in spite of *Daed*'s insistence that the dog was the reason he'd fallen in the kitchen.

Or maybe it was simply that Mandy felt comfortable with her *grossdawdi* and wanted to spend time with him. Leah was startled to remember when she'd done the same. *Mamm* used to call her "Abram's little shadow." Back then, Leah had been annoyed when she had to go inside and help with chores in the house rather than in the barns and fields as Johnny did. Those days seemed forever ago, a life that wasn't part of hers anymore.

And recalling that made her very sad. She knew the exact moment when her relationship with her *daed* changed. The special closeness she'd shared with *Daed* died the first time he sent back her letter unopened. That day, as she stood in front of the mailbox in the apartment lobby and held the envelope with the words Return to

Sender scrawled in *Daed*'s bold handwriting across the front, she'd felt as if her own *daed* had become a stranger. Her loving *daed* wouldn't ever make her choose a side. She couldn't choose either Johnny or her *daed*. It was impossible. Johnny and Mandy needed her too much for her to turn her back on them. The chasm between her and her *daed* widened with every passing year and every letter that was returned.

"I'm sorry, Leah." Mandy's voice jerked Leah out of her thoughts. The little girl flushed, then dug her bare toe into the grass by the fence. "I'm sorry if I upset you and *Grossmammi*, but I don't understand. Why can't I walk across the field by myself to come to see *Mamm Millich*? It's not like I'm a baby, and it's just a field way out here in the boonies. If Isabella's mother lets her take the bus to the Philadelphia Museum of Art by herself, why can't I come over here by myself?"

No matter how Isabella bragged, Leah was certain that Mrs. Martinez never allowed her nine-year-old daughter to travel through the city on a bus alone. From what she'd observed, Mrs. Martinez hovered around her daughter constantly, seldom giving the girl a chance to make any decisions for herself. Trying to tell Mandy that Isabella wasn't being honest would be a waste of time. Her niece believed the fantastic stories.

"I know you're sorry, Mandy, and I'm sorry, too. You did what I've asked you to. You let a grown-up know where you were going. I should have checked with everyone before I rushed to look for you." She took her niece's hand and squeezed it. "Will you forgive me?"

"You're asking me if *I* will forgive *you*?"

"It's our way to ask forgiveness and to give it," came

Ezra's voice. "A person can't expect to be forgiven if he or she isn't willing to forgive."

She looked over Mandy's head to see him on the other side of the fence. He carried a shovel and wore knee-high barn boots coated with dirt and hay, but he was more handsome than any *Englischer* with a fancy suit. His straw hat shaded his face, but his arms beneath his rolled-up sleeves were already deep tan from his time in the fields.

Caught up in her conversation with her niece, she hadn't heard him approach. She was glad that he had interjected such sensible words into the conversation.

"For the Amish, it is the core of our relationship with God," he went on, smiling at the little girl, who gazed up at him as she listened intently. "Do you remember what the bishop preached last church Sunday?"

"*Ja*. He said that we need to forgive a bunch of times," Mandy said. "Seven times…something."

"That's right. You really were listening."

She beamed at his praise, and Leah couldn't help thinking what a *gut daed* Ezra would be. He was patient and, like Esther at school, he pushed *kinder* to think for themselves. Mandy respected him, as his nephews and niece did, because he offered them respect in return. Equally important, he was steadfast in his faith, showing them his gentle strength came from God.

"The verses are from the Book of Luke," Ezra went on. "'If thy brother trespass against thee, rebuke him; and if he repent, forgive him. And if he trespass against thee seven times in a day, and seven times in a day turn again to thee, saying, I repent; thou shalt forgive him.' If I want God to forgive one of His *kinder*—me, for example—I need to forgive His other *kinder*."

Mandy considered the words, then grinned. "That makes sense." Looking up at Leah, she said, "I forgive you, Leah. I know you worry about me because you love me."

"And I forgive you, Mandy. You did what we asked you to, which shows that you're growing up to be a responsible young lady." When Mandy threw her arms around Leah, she hugged her niece, grateful that the little girl was part of her life.

Ezra's smile broadened. "Now that is settled, to what do I owe the pleasure of a visit from two such lovely ladies?"

As her niece giggled at his question, Leah looked at the top rail and realized he'd leaned his hand on it close to hers. Even though it was impossible, she was sure she could feel warmth from his rough skin. He could slip his hand over hers easily, as he'd done before the auction. He didn't shift his hand, and she pushed her disappointment down deep.

"I came over to see *Mamm Millich*," said Mandy. "Where is she?"

"Resting," he replied.

"Can I see her?"

"Only if you promise to be quiet and make no sudden moves. Her calf will be born soon, so she needs all the rest she can get right now. After the calf comes, she will be busy taking care of it."

Mandy's nose wrinkled. "I remember when Isabella's baby brother was born. He always needed something." Abruptly her mood shifted to melancholy. "I wish I had a brother or sister."

"Our family is big, I don't think anyone would notice if you want to be an honorary part of it," Ezra said, wink-

ing at Leah. "Then you'd have more brothers and sisters than you probably want."

"Can I?" She whirled to Leah. "Can I be part of Ezra's family?"

"As long as..." she replied, putting her hands on her niece's shoulders and trying not to laugh at how seriously Mandy was taking Ezra's jest, "you stay part of mine, too."

"But you can be an honorary part of Ezra's family, too. You'd like that, right, Ezra?"

Leah pulled in a sharp breath. She couldn't look at him. Not when she was sure her face was turning a brilliant red. Becoming a part of Ezra's family had implications that had lately filled her dreams, but which she hadn't dared to think about while awake. The dreams weren't very different from the ones she'd had as a teenager when she imagined Ezra asking if he could take her home from a singing. He'd had plenty of chances, but, until the night he kissed her, she thought he didn't want to risk their friendship if a courtship didn't work out.

"Let's try it with you first, Mandy," Ezra said, his voice light and filled with amusement. "Three sisters may be enough for me."

"Okay." Mandy gave her another hug and giggled. "Sorry, Leah. I got the last spot in the Stoltzfus family."

"You did." Leah focused on her niece, not ready to meet Ezra's gaze yet.

When he told them to meet him in the lower level of the barn, she hoped she'd have her emotions back under control by the time she and Mandy got there. She let Mandy babble about seeing the pregnant cow and how she and Ezra's niece Deborah would be honorary cous-

ins now. Maybe her niece would be willing to miss the birthday party in Philadelphia now.

Looking back across the field, she saw *Mamm* walking to the barn. To check on *Daed*, no doubt. Leah waved to her *mamm* and smiled when *Mamm* waved back to her and Mandy. Knowing that Mandy had been found would ease *Mamm*'s mind, but Leah wished her *daed* would see how much his refusal to acknowledge his need to see a doctor was weighing on his wife.

Leah needed to lighten Mamm's burden instead of worrying about herself. God must have some reason for bringing her back to Paradise Springs at the precise time when her stubborn *daed* and fearful *mamm* needed her help.

Her steps were lighter when she stepped into the musky shadows in the barn. She had a purpose for her life again: to find the best way to help *Daed* and *Mamm* through this uncertain time. Until now, she hadn't realized how adrift she'd been since Johnny died. God had guided her to the place she needed to be.

"You're smiling, Aunt Leah," Mandy said as she swung their clasped hands between them.

"It's because I'm spending time with my favorite niece."

"Your *only* niece," she corrected as she did each time Leah said that.

"My favorite and only niece. How's that?"

"Perfect!"

Ahead of them, Ezra stood beside a stall with its door shut. His expression as he gazed over the wall was gentle and caring. Her heart skipped several times as she saw the honest happiness on his face. Being a farmer was the perfect life for him. He loved tending to the animals and the land that had been in his family for generations. As

he'd told her when it was first discussed years ago that he would take over the farm, he was a caretaker who must ensure the land and buildings were in excellent shape for the generations to come.

"Ezra?" she called quietly.

He straightened and motioned for them to come closer. Holding his finger to his lips, he inched back so Mandy could press up against the stall and, standing on tiptoe, peek over it. She squirmed in excitement but didn't squeal as Leah guessed she wanted to.

"She's fat," Mandy whispered.

"That happens when a cow is about to have a calf," he replied with a throaty chuckle. "Leah, do you want to see, too?"

Before she could answer, he put his hand at the back of her waist to guide her between him and the stall. Warmth spread through her and lingered, even when he drew his fingers away. His breath caressed her nape as he leaned forward to answer her niece's questions. When he gestured, she felt surrounded by him. She needed only to lean her head back an inch or two, and it would settle against his shoulder. Closing her eyes, she drew in a deep breath flavored with the aroma of him, a mixture of freshly cut hay and his own unique scent.

Her eyes popped open when Ezra said, "That's enough for now." She wanted to protest it wasn't, though she knew he wasn't talking about them being close to each other. He wanted to make sure the cow wasn't disturbed by having too many visitors for too long.

"Bye, *Mamm Millich*." Mandy blew the cow a kiss before pushing back from the stall. Waiting until they were a few steps away, she asked, "Can I come back to see her again?"

"Maybe you should wait until the calf is born," Leah

said quickly. "As Ezra said, *Mamm Millich* needs her rest now."

"Will you call me the minute the calf is born?"

"Maybe not the exact minute, but I will let you know." He chuckled. "I'll need help giving the calf a name, so I'd appreciate it if you came up with some."

Mandy started to clap in excitement, then glanced back at the stall. Lowering her hands, she said, "I'll make a list of *gut* names."

"In the meantime," he said with another wink that set Leah's heart speeding again, "I know a secret. The calico barn cat has kittens hidden in the haymow."

"Kittens! How many?"

"Four, I think. She's kept them hidden pretty well until the last couple of days. If you look under the tarp on the old buggy up there, you may find them."

She tugged on Leah's arm. "Can I?"

"Go ahead, but remember they're babies. Handle them very carefully."

"I will!" She ran out the door to go up into the haymow.

As Leah started to follow, Ezra asked, "Can I talk to you? Alone?"

She couldn't avoid looking at him any longer. His *gut* humor had vanished, and his expression was as serious as a deacon scolding a misbehaving member. "As long as it's quick. I need to get back home to help *Mamm*."

"This shouldn't take long."

She wondered what *this* was; then she wondered if she really wanted to know when her feelings were on such a seesaw.

Why was Leah looking distressed? She hadn't reacted as he'd expected recently. He was trying to take Joshua's

advice and be straightforward, but that didn't seem to be working very well. He didn't know what else to do, so he plunged on.

"Are you all right?" he asked.

"I'm *gut*." A wobbly smile returned to her face. "Now."

"You seemed pretty shaken up out by the fence."

"I was when *Mamm* came to me to find out if I'd seen Mandy recently. I should have known right away that she'd be over here visiting her favorite cow."

"And that's all it was?"

"Isn't that enough?"

"Ja." Enough for other people, but not enough to make Leah Beiler agitated. As she'd shown again when Rose became hysterical after Isaiah was named the new minister, Leah could easily deal with a crisis.

"What did you want to talk to me about?"

"Cheese."

"Cheese?" Her bafflement appeared genuine. "I thought you had to wait until *Mamm Millich* freshened and started giving milk after her calf is born."

"I'm milking a couple of the other Brown Swiss, so I thought I'd experiment with a mixture of their milk and the other cows' for now. Do you want to try it? My *mamm* says the best thing to make someone less upset is to give them something to eat."

"Mine says the same thing."

"What was it that you used to say? That they got together and came up with sayings to teach us identical lessons."

"I don't remember saying that, but it does sound like something I'd say." She glanced up as she heard Mandy's quick steps in the haymow overhead. "I don't want to leave Mandy alone in the barn."

"You won't. I've been doing my cheese-making down here in a room off the milking parlor. *Mamm* and Esther got tired of my experimenting in their kitchen, especially when it was time to make meals. This way…" He led her through the milking parlor. Opening a door, he stepped to one side so she could enter first.

He heard her soft gasp, and he smiled. Only his family had come into the rooms he'd equipped with everything he needed to make cheese, and they had been as awed as Leah was.

"Tell me what it does." She touched the side of the spotless vat right in front of them. It was five feet long and about two feet deep. Both sides slanted down slightly to a gutter that ran the length of the rectangular vat.

Ezra didn't try to hide his enthusiasm as he explained that the vat was where the process began. He pointed to nearby shelves and the containers that held either salt or the rennet that would turn the milk into curds when it was slowly heated. Ducking under the hoses that hung from metal rods that went from one side of the room to the other, he showed her which ones brought milk in from the storage tank. The others supplied water for when he cleaned the equipment. He took her step-by-step through the cheese-making process, starting with separating the solidifying cheese curds from the liquid whey, which was drained from the vat and saved to be used as fertilizer on the farm's cornfields.

"It's *gut* for a couple of years, then I'll have to add another application," he said.

He showed her the curds knife that cut the curds into small cubes. It was as wide as the vat and constructed of small wires so the curds could be cut to the bottom. Salt and flavoring were added before the cheese was

put in a press where pressure squeezed out the rest of the whey over the next day. He opened another door and showed her the wooden racks where the cheese was then left to age.

"The longer it's aged, the stronger the flavor." He picked up a rectangle of cheese and carried it to a table. "This block is sage cheddar. Want a bite?" He kept his expression even so she could not guess how much he wanted—and valued—her opinion.

She smiled. "*Ja*, but only if you've improved since your first attempts." She glanced around, and he guessed she was remembering when he used to hang cheesecloth bags with draining cheese from the rafters.

"It could not taste worse."

"I agree."

He cut a chunk of the fragrant cheese and offered it to her. When she took it, thanking him, he started to slice another piece. He kept his gaze on her as she took a hearty bite of the cheese. She had never been one of those girls who was afraid to try something new, whether it was swinging out over a pond on a tire hung from a tree or an unfamiliar food.

Memories of time he'd spent with Leah poured through his head. Whether he was awake or asleep, the image of her face or the memory of something she had said filled his mind.

Her brows rose, and she smiled again as she said, "Ezra, this is definitely an improvement from the last time I tasted your cheese."

"Freshly turned soil would be taste better than those first attempts of mine did, so I'm not sure if you like it or not."

"It's *gut*. Very *gut*."

"Danki," he said. What else could he say? *Will you let me kiss you again so I can see if our lips together are as sweet as I remember?*

"Can I have another piece?"

"If you eat it all now, there won't be any for me to take to the market this fall once the harvesting is done." He sliced another generous piece and held it out to her. When she took it, he added, "You've been to the market in Philadelphia, haven't you? Did you see anything there to help me make my cheese stand out from other vendors at the Central Market in Lancaster? If I can persuade people to buy it, I'm hopeful that they'll come back for more, but it's getting them to select my cheese instead of the cheese at another display."

He realized he was babbling like a *blabbermaul.* His family and neighbors would be shocked to hear a man who spoke with measured words chattering like an annoyed squirrel.

"This means so much to you," she said as she broke off a small corner of the piece he'd given her. "I'm happy you're having a chance to make your dream come true." She popped the morsel into her mouth, then yelped as the door opened into her back.

Mandy poked her head in and stared. "Here you are. What's this stuff?" She stepped into the room.

"It's where Ezra makes and stores his cheese," Leah replied as she handed her niece half of the piece she had remaining.

"Cool!" Mandy took a bite and grinned. "This is yummy, Ezra."

"Did you find the kittens?" he asked, wishing she'd been delayed a few minutes more before she came back to the lower level.

"I did! They're cute, cute, cute! Do you think *Grossdawdi* would let me have one?"

"Ezra needs those kittens to grow up and hunt mice in the barn. We have cats at home."

"But not kittens!"

Ezra chuckled as he looked at Leah over the little girl's head. "You can't argue with that."

"I can't wait," Mandy went on, so excited she bounced from one foot to the other, "to tell Isabella about the cows, the kittens and Ezra's cheese. She's going to wish she had a chance to visit a farm, too."

Leah's face stiffened as her niece spoke easily of leaving Paradise Springs, and he wondered if his face was as taut. He waited for Leah to answer Mandy, to tell her they were going to stay here, but she didn't.

All she said was a quick *"danki"* before she took Mandy's hand and bade him a *gut* day. They were gone before he had a chance to reply.

Chapter Ten

Ezra stopped his buggy by the bridge at the edge of the village as his eye was caught by a motion on the bank of the stream below it. Chipped concrete walls showed where vehicles had struck the old bridge. The walkway on the far side of the walls had been fenced off because it was no longer safe. As for the bridge itself, there was some concern it could continue to support a fully loaded milk truck. The farms between it and Gordonville depended on that truck to take their milk to the processing plant about twenty miles to the west. That was one of the reasons he had decided to start experimenting with making his own cheese before he had more Brown Swiss cows in his herd.

Getting out, he looped the reins over the wooden slats that blocked the walkway. An easy leap over the railing dropped him down onto the grassy slope. Leah stood at the bottom on the stony shore. She was fishing patiently in the fast-moving water. An open creel basket and long-handled net sat by her bare feet. Her black sneakers and socks were safely away from the water.

"Any luck?" he called as he got closer.

With a wave, she motioned him to come down. He hadn't been sure if she would after their conversation yesterday had ended abruptly. He half walked, half slid down toward the stream.

"Look!" She pointed at the woven willow basket. "I've caught three nice trout already. When *Mamm* said she'd like some fish, I decided to sneak away after Mandy got home from school and see what I could catch. I hope to hook one more. If I get my full limit of five, that would be *gut*, but four should be enough for us for supper."

"Mind if I watch?"

Surprise blossomed in her eyes, but she said, "If you want."

Sitting on the edge of the grass, he was quiet as she waited for a bite. He moved only when her line went taut. As she fought with the fish to bring it ashore, he picked up the net. She glanced at him and nodded. He had the net ready when she reeled the fish up out of the water. It was more than a foot long, and it must have weighed, he guessed, close to two pounds.

"Nice one," he said as he lifted it from the net and carefully undid the hook. He placed the fish in the creel before handing the line back to her so she could continue.

When she tossed the line back into the stream close to where she'd caught the other fish, he sat again. He was quiet once more and took the time to admire how the strands of blond hair that had escaped from her *kapp* glistened in the sunlight. Her pretty mouth was slightly open, and a corner of her tongue peeked out as she waited eagerly for the next bite. Her dimple was only faintly visible on her left cheek. He was sure he had never seen a sight more beautiful than she was as she reveled in the game between her and the fish.

How could she ever have been happy in Philadelphia? He'd been there once many years ago, and he recalled the streets where nothing green grew except in flower boxes on the houses. Even the sun was banned on the ground around the tallest buildings. He'd gone past both the Delaware and the Schuylkill Rivers, and he hadn't seen any place where a person could toss a line in the water in the hope of hooking a fish.

Her line tightened again quickly, and he rose to hold the net up to snag the fish as soon as it was out of the water. It was always disappointing when the fish threw the hook and escaped at the last minute.

"Danki," she said when he released the line after unhooking the fish. She looked into the creel. "That should be enough for tonight, and I'd better head home if I want to get them cleaned and cooked for supper."

"Next time you go fishing, ask me to come along."

"Really?"

"I wouldn't have said so if I didn't mean it." He flipped the top of the creel closed and lifted it by the shoulder strap, holding it out far enough so any water didn't splash on his boots. "Why don't you believe me?"

Leah didn't give him a quick answer. Instead, she went to where she'd left her shoes and socks and, leaning her pole against the slope, pulled them on. She looked up at him.

"Forgive me, Ezra. You've never given me any reason to disbelieve you. I appreciate you always being honest with me."

He was glad when she turned her attention to tying her sneakers so she didn't see his expression. Though he tried to keep his smile in place, he knew it must look grotesque. He hadn't always been honest with her. He had

been too scared to tell her years ago that he wanted to court her to discover if friendship really could become love. What would she say now if she knew that his faith had weakened since she left? Or that he was afraid of asking a simple question—*Are you staying?*—because the answer could be no.

"I wish everyone would be as honest," she continued when he didn't answer. "Some act as if I'm hiding horrible secrets about my life while I was away."

"It might have been easier if folks knew where you'd gone before you came back."

She came to her feet. "They could have asked *Daed.* He knew."

"He did?" He picked up her rod. "How?"

"My return address was on the letters I wrote to him almost every week while we were gone."

"You wrote to him? Every week?"

Tears glistened in her eyes. *"Ja."*

Something didn't make sense. As he walked up the slope beside her, he asked, "How did Abram keep from sharing the news of Johnny's accident or Mandy's birth? I'm amazed Fannie could keep from saying anything to *Mamm.*"

"She didn't know about the accident or Mandy. Neither did *Daed.*" Her voice broke as she whispered, "He returned my letters unopened."

Ezra mouthed the word *unopened*, but no sound emerged past his shock. Abram Beiler had always been a stern *daed* and a stubborn man. In spite of that, Ezra had never doubted that he loved his *kinder*. How could any man turn his back on his *kinder* completely? Most Amish *daeds* tried to locate their *kinder* who had jumped

the fence and went to them, urging them to come home. Abram had never gone to Philadelphia as far as Ezra knew.

"Neither *Daed* nor Johnny could relent and admit they'd been wrong to let their anger take their quarrels so far." Leah's words remained hushed. "And neither of them was willing to be the first to ask for or offer forgiveness. Maybe *Daed* forgave Johnny, but Johnny couldn't forgive him." She pressed her hands to her face. "I pray that, in his final moments, Johnny found peace by granting *Daed* the forgiveness that God has given freely to us. I can't stand the idea that he went to God with that burden on his soul."

He set the creel basket and fishing rod on the grass. Slowly, knowing what he risked, he drew her quivering hands down from her face. Seeing the torment in her purple eyes was like having a knife driven into his heart.

Lord, help me find the words to help Leah. You have given me this opportunity to ease her anguish. Now please give me the words.

He took a deep breath before he said, "In spite of the fact that Johnny made plenty of bad decisions, your brother wasn't a bad person. He was generous and a *gut* friend to those he counted as his friends. He cared deeply for the animals in his care, and his love for you never wavered. He wouldn't tolerate bullies, whether they were plain or *Englisch*. One time, I saw him stick up for a younger boy against a couple of louts who were bigger than Johnny was. He never flinched when they threatened to beat him to a pulp. He simply stood there between them and the *kind* until they walked away."

"I didn't know that."

"He never spoke of it after it happened. Even Abram

knew that Johnny had a *gut* heart, though he was frustrated by your brother's wild spirit."

"I wish I could believe that. I haven't heard *Daed* speak Johnny's name once. It's as if he wishes Johnny was never born." Her voice caught. "And me."

Lord, Ezra prayed silently, *if it is Your will, help Leah and her* daed. *If I'm not Your instrument of change in their lives, bring someone else into her life who can open her* daed*'s heart so he will reveal how special she is to him.*

Aloud, he said, "That's not true. Abram was as devastated as your *mamm* was when you two disappeared. Even if he doesn't let you or anyone else see it now, I witnessed his pain right after you left, and I know it was real." As she opened her mouth to protest, he quickly added, "It doesn't matter what we think. God knows what is in our hearts, and He judges us on that. He knows the depth of your *daed*'s love for his *kinder*—all his *kinder*!—and he knows the true reasons that kept Johnny from coming home."

She blinked back tears. "*Danki*, Ezra. I needed that reminder of God's love. I should have known that I could talk to you about anything, even how *Daed* can't forgive me for leaving."

He realized he really didn't want to talk. He wanted to gaze into Leah's shining eyes. He wanted to do more than that. If he drew her into his arms now, would she pull away again or would she come willingly? Did she guess how often she was in his thoughts?

"What about you, Ezra? Have you forgiven me for leaving?"

"Certainly." His voice caught, and he cleared his tight throat. "Though from what you've said since your return,

there seems to be nothing to forgive you for other than loving your brother too much."

"Can anyone love a brother too much?"

He tilted his hat back and swiped a hand across his brow. "I don't have an answer for that because I've never faced the choice you did."

"But you believe I was silly to follow Johnny blindly."

"I don't think you followed him blindly. You wanted to save him from himself. Abram might have given up on him, but you never did."

"He's my twin." She gulped and stared at the ground. "He *was* my twin."

He cupped her chin and tipped her face up so she couldn't hide it from him. "Johnny is still your twin. Eventually you will be reunited." He lifted one corner of his mouth in the best smile he could manage. "I hope that isn't for a long time to come."

"I miss him." Her voice broke on the few words.

"I can't imagine what it must be like to lose a twin."

"Is the void in my life any greater than if I lost someone else I love? I wouldn't say greater. It's different. More like a part of myself died along with him. He was always there, even from before I can remember."

"Me, too." He sighed in a mixture of sorrow and discouragement as she stepped away after stirring memories he had tried to submerge for longer than she'd been gone.

"What happened with you and Johnny?" she asked, again proving that she was privy to his thoughts even when he didn't speak them. "One day, you were the best of friends, and then, the next, he acted as if you didn't exist."

"You don't know?" He doubted there was anything she could have said that would have surprised him more.

Picking up the rod and creel, he started up the slope again. "I was sure Johnny told you how he believed I'd betrayed him."

"No. He only said that he'd been *dumm* to consider you a friend. He didn't say anything else. Why would he think you betrayed him?"

Even now, the hurt Ezra had suffered burst forth, as strong as when it was fresh. "At least you didn't ask me if I betrayed him."

"I know both of you." She didn't add anything more.

Climbing over the guardrail, he leaned the rod against the side of the buggy and set the creel on the ground beside it. He turned to assist Leah over the metal rail, but she'd already managed by herself. He swallowed his disappointment, because he had been looking forward to putting his hands on her slender waist, lifting her over and bringing her down right in front of him.

"It happened a long time ago," he said. "I'm not sure resurrecting it is a *gut* idea."

"I'm not asking you to speak ill of the dead. Tell me what happened."

He rested his arm on the buggy and watched as a car swept by and over the bridge, heading toward town at a speed too high for the winding road. The bright red car looked like the one that was often parked in the yard of the house next to his brother Joshua's house.

"Ezra?" Leah prompted.

He couldn't deny her the truth. "It started with plans that some of the older kids, the ones on their *rumspringa*, made to go to Hersheypark."

"Lots of kids go to the amusement park during their *rumspringa* years."

"And they talk about the rides and how much fun they

are and the food and the other amusements." He looked at her directly when he said, "Johnny really wanted to go. So much that when he heard the Hershberger brothers weren't going, he decided we should."

"But you were boys then, too young for a *rumspringa* trip."

"Ja." He sighed. "I told Johnny that, but he wouldn't listen. He kept trying to persuade me to go with them. They believed that the van driver wouldn't notice we were younger than the other kids because *Englischers* have a hard time telling us apart when we're wearing our straw hats and shirts of the same color."

"Them? Who else?"

"Do you remember Steven McMurray? The *Englisch* boy who lived on the farm about a mile down the road toward Gordonville?"

She frowned as she nodded. "He was always getting in trouble. Johnny thought he was great. Whatever happened to him?"

"He's the police chief in Paradise Springs now." He chuckled when she stared at him. "Who would have guessed that the same boy who talked your brother into trying to sneak off to Hersheypark would now be doing a *gut* job of keeping the peace? Maybe he's always one step ahead of the kids because he always was in the middle of trouble himself growing up."

"Johnny and Steven planned to sneak onto the van?"

"Ja, and they invited me to go with them. When I said I didn't think their plan would work and I wanted no part of it, they told me I was a coward."

"That is when you stopped being friends?"

In the light coming through the leaves on the trees along the road, he could see her holding her lower lip be-

tween her teeth, waiting for his answer. He would have liked to say it was, that he—rather than Johnny—had brought about the end of their friendship, but he wouldn't lie to her.

"It was later, Leah," he said sadly. "After their scheme was discovered, Johnny accused me of tattling on them. He believed it was my fault they got caught, even though the driver refused to let them get in the van because he saw they were too young. The driver contacted Abram and Steven's *daed*, and they both came to collect their sons. I was told that by Joshua, who went on their trip."

"I didn't know." She crossed her arms in front of her. "Even then, Johnny and *Daed* were arguing so often that I'd stopped listening to what they were quarreling about."

"He told me I'd be sorry that I betrayed him, and he didn't like when I turned my back on him and walked away."

"It must have been after that when Johnny became furious that you and I were still friends."

"But you remained my friend."

"Johnny and I are twins, not the same person. We often had different opinions." Her eyes rose to meet his gaze. "I'm sorry he felt he had to end your friendship. He paid a high cost for fulfilling his threat. Johnny never was able to forget what he saw as a slight. He held on to grudges, even though it only hurt him. I loved him, but I wasn't blind to how he couldn't turn the other cheek. He sought revenge, instead, waiting weeks or months if he had to."

Or years? Johnny must have known for a fact that Leah would go with him to plead with him to come back from the *Englisch* world. Shock rushed through Ezra. Had Johnny lured his sister away, being aware that while

his leaving would hurt Abram, Leah going would be even more painful for his *daed*…and for Ezra?

It was a heinous thought, and he should be praying for forgiveness for even allowing it to form. Yet he couldn't help believing there was some truth in his suspicions. Maybe Johnny hadn't made his plans to leave with such a goal in his mind, but the result had been the same.

"Being angry now is useless." She put her hand on his bare forearm. "It's time to let the past go."

"I agree." He splayed his fingers across her cheek, savoring the warmth the sun had burnished into her skin. As he touched her, confirming that she really stood in front of him, he realized how much he had harbored the fear that none of this was anything more than a dream. That she hadn't truly come back. His own yearning to see her had created a realistic dream.

He had been thinking about their one kiss more and more often. But he was startled by how he didn't want only to kiss her. He longed to bring her into his arms and cradle her close as he lost himself in her amazing eyes while her loosened hair fell in a golden cascade down over his hands.

The thought should have startled him even more than his doubts about her twin, but it didn't. Since the year he turned seventeen and really started noticing girls and realizing that eventually he needed to choose one to marry, there had been only one he'd considered.

Leah Beiler.

He had taken other girls home in his courting buggy, but he'd asked each of them *after* Leah accepted another guy's invitation. At the time, he'd been too worried about ruining their friendship to ask if he might court her.

What a fool he'd been!

He'd been even a greater fool her last night in Paradise Springs. If he'd told her that night how he felt, would she have stayed in Paradise Springs to be with him, or would she have run away with her brother in an effort to save Johnny from himself?

But she was home now, and perhaps if he gave her a *gut* reason to stay, she would remain here. As he tipped her face toward him, her lovely eyes closed in an invitation to kiss her. An invitation he would gladly accept.

Leah jumped away from him as another car approached the bridge. She grabbed her fishing pole and creel. "I should get these fish cleaned before they go bad, and I promised *Mamm* that I'd get the mail so she didn't have to leave..." As her voice trailed into silence, she looked down at her creel.

She might be checking the fish in it, but he guessed she was trying to avoid revealing something she was keeping a secret. What? Something about the mail? Had Mandy received another invitation to Philadelphia? Had Leah?

"I'll give you a ride home, if you'd like," he said, hoping she would open up on the short journey.

She nodded and handed him her fishing equipment. As he moved to put it in the storage area behind the buggy's cab, she climbed in by herself.

He hoped it was only because she was in a hurry to get her catch home. Thinking of the alternatives was too painful.

Leah let happiness enfold her as Ezra kept silence from filling the buggy. When he began talking about how Esther planned to have a work frolic for the scholars' families at the school, she let him keep the conversation light

and on something that was part of their present. The past was over, and she wanted to enjoy that she and Ezra were chatting with an ease she had been unsure they'd ever regain. His arm brushed hers as he drew on the reins to slow the horse before turning into the lane leading to her *daed*'s farm.

It was tempting to take his hand, but she didn't want to do anything to disrupt the easy peace that had settled between them. With the birds chirping in the trees along the road and the late-afternoon sun warm on the buggy, she sent up a silent prayer of gratitude to God for the *wunderbaar* day He had given them.

"'This is the day which the Lord hath made, we will rejoice and be glad in it,'" Ezra said.

She swiveled on the seat to face him. "I was thinking the same thing."

"Great minds."

"Or great faith."

He sighed. "I'm working on that."

"Me, too."

"You? You rush in where others fear to tread without thought of what you might encounter."

"Maybe I need to think a little bit more before I jump in."

"Maybe you should." His voice had a hushed roughness that sent a tingle of delight through her. Drawing back on the reins, he smiled when she asked why they were stopping. "You said you needed to get the mail on your way home."

"I'm glad *you* remembered." She used humor to cover her shock that she could have forgotten how she had told *Mamm* she'd collect the mail so her *mamm* and Mandy could remain close to *Daed* in case he fell again.

"Let me." He stretched to open the mailbox. Gathering the mail inside, he handed it to her.

"Danki." She flipped through the envelopes and paused at two thicker ones. "Oh, *Mamm* will be pleased. There are two of her circle letters. One from her sister and the other from mine."

Her *mamm* had been writing these round-robin letters all of Leah's life. It was a simple system where each person wrote about the new events in her life and, after taking out the page with her previous note, mailed it to the next name in the circle. Usually it took about a month for each letter to complete its circle, so some of the news was stale while other bits were very recent.

Below the envelope from her sister was another with her name typed on it. "I wonder who's sending me a letter."

"From where?"

She looked at the postmark. "Philadelphia."

His shoulders straightened beside her, and tension radiated off him like heat from a stove.

Why hadn't she thought before she blurted out the answer? Ezra seemed to react that way whenever the city was mentioned. Quickly Leah checked the return address and smiled.

"It's from Mrs. Whittaker," she said, "the owner of the shop where I sold my quilts in Philadelphia." She opened the envelope and drew out the single, folded sheet inside.

"You don't need to read the letter. I'll tell you what it says. She'd like more of your quilts." Ezra's tone became more relaxed as he urged the horse forward again.

She looked up, surprised. *"Ja,* but how did you know?"

"I have seen your work, Leah. It's beautiful, and I'm

sure she'd like having more of your quilts to sell in her shop."

"I doubt I could make enough to sell in her shop and also in Amos's store."

"You may earn more in Philadelphia because city folks seem to have more money than country folk."

"But people come to Lancaster County to find quilts made by plain seamstresses. Oh!" she added as she continued to read. "She wants me to come to Philadelphia and teach a series of classes in quilting."

"I am sure you would have enjoyed that. I remember you teaching Esther to love quilting."

"Would have enjoyed? Why do you assume that I won't go?"

Again his shoulders grew taut. "Are you considering it?"

"Her offer is generous, and I'm sure I could arrange to go at the same time Mandy wants to attend Isabella's party."

"You make it sound easy to leave." His accusation lashed her like a fiery rope.

"What's wrong? If I go to Philadelphia, it doesn't mean I'll stay there."

"Mandy wants to, and you won't let her stay there alone."

"I'm her guardian. I'll decide where she needs to be."

"Even if she's unhappy here? As unhappy as her *daed* was?"

Reaching past him, Leah tugged on the reins to stop the buggy in the middle of the lane. She jumped down and snatched her fishing rod and creel out of the back. She looked up at him as she said, "I don't know how to answer your questions, Ezra. They plague me every night

and keep me awake. I've been praying for guidance, but I haven't gotten an answer yet. However, I do know that *I* have plenty reasons of my own for coming back."

"What are they?"

She saw the raw vulnerability on his face, and, for a moment, she considered saying he was one of the reasons. If she did, he might ask her about the others. So all she did was thank him for the ride. She couldn't reveal how concerned she was with *Daed*'s spells of dizziness and the falls that left him bruised. *Mamm* had asked her to keep the information to herself, and, even though she hated being caught up in more secrets, she wouldn't break that trust.

Not again.

Chapter Eleven

Ezra finished unharnessing the mules and leaving them to graze. They deserved rest after the long day of working in the field, turning the hay so it dried evenly. Tomorrow's work would be even harder if the hay was dry enough to bale. He always was cautious with drying the hay. If even a bit of moisture remained, the compressed bale could generate heat leading to spontaneous combustion. Almost every summer, a barn burned in Lancaster County or one of the surrounding counties because a farmer was too impatient and put his hay in green.

Had he been too impatient with Leah yesterday? He couldn't mistake her excitement when she read the letter from the *Englisch* lady. She'd been pleased that she had an excuse to go back to Philadelphia with Mandy. She'd said she had reasons for coming back, but were they more important to her than her niece's happiness?

Instantly he felt the guilt that had come in the wake of too many of his thoughts in the past few weeks. Leah should be praised for her willingness to sacrifice her life here in Paradise Springs because of her dedication to her niece.

Yet he wished she'd explained the reasons that had brought her home. He hadn't expected her to say his name, but he'd hoped she would. Even if he were one of them, what were the others and why wouldn't she reveal them?

"Stop it!" he grumbled. The same thoughts had chased him up and down the length of the field all day, and he hadn't come up with a single answer.

Leah had spoken to him about how she treasured their friendship. Was he supposed to take that as a signal she was satisfied with their relationship, as she had been when they were younger?

"Stop it! Think of something you *can* do something about."

He tried, focusing on the rest of the day's chores. He went into the lower level of the barn and to the sink. Picking up the ladle from the water bucket beside the sink, he primed the pump and pushed its handle until icy water rushed out. He washed the sweat from his face.

His mouth felt as dry and dusty as the field. As he wiped his hands, he decided to go into the house and get some iced tea before he brought the cows in for milking. Maybe he could grab a couple of cookies to wolf down without *Mamm* warning him that he'd ruin his supper. As hard as he'd worked today and as little as he'd slept last night, he felt as if he could eat his way through the canned food in the cellar and still be hungry.

Ezra stopped by *Mamm Millich*'s stall and folded his arms on the door. She was on her feet and eating without any signs of discomfort. With a first calf, it was likely to come very early or very late.

"As long as it comes healthy," he said as he ran his hand over the cow's back. "And you stay healthy, too."

She didn't look at him, simply kept eating. With a chuckle, he walked through milking parlor to the outside door. He drew in deep breaths of the thick scents of animals and feed along with the faint odor of aging cheese. For years, that combination had been the sweetest perfume he could imagine.

Until Leah returned, and he drank in the aromas of her soap and shampoo. It was more intoxicating than even the beer he'd tried on his short *rumspringa*. Now she was talking easily of leaving again.

He didn't bother to scold himself to think of something else. No matter how hard he tried, his thoughts found a way to wind back to her.

Ezra strode out and climbed the hill to the lane and the house on the other side of it. When he reached the top, he stopped and stared at his brothers, who were gathered in a semicircle in front of the upper barn door. All six of them were there, and each one stood with his hands clasped in front of him. They resembled a row of cornstalks on a windless day, for none of them moved a muscle as he approached.

"What's going on?" he asked.

"We need to speak with you, Ezra," announced Joshua in a tone that sounded like the coming of doom.

He pushed forward, trying to guess why they stood there. If something *wunderbaar* had happened, Esther would be there. Probably *Mamm*, as well.

Something bad?

Their faces were as somber as if they were on their way to Sunday services, but he didn't see the weight of bad news heavy on their shoulders. In fact, his youngest brother's eyes twinkled with suppressed merriment. What was going on?

As if he'd asked that question again, Amos and Micah stepped forward, and their other brothers closed up the spaces they'd left. Amos moved to Ezra's right and Micah to his left. They grasped his arms and led him toward the barn.

"Don't I get to know what's going on?" he asked.

"Nope," said Amos and Micah at the same time as they kept him moving directly toward the rest of their brothers who moved aside at the last minute. As his younger brothers steered Ezra into the barn, the others, except for Joshua, followed in silence.

Sunlight shone through the barn, making dust motes dance as they did in the sunlight cascading through the windows high under the roof. He noticed that in the second before a gleam caught his eye.

In front of him, in the very center of the space where the podium had stood for the mud sale, was an open buggy. Its single seat had room for two adults. *Daed* had given it to him after his sixteenth birthday, and it was one of the first buggies Joshua had built during his apprenticeship in a buggy shop near Strasburg. For years, the buggy had lurked in a back corner out of the way. Ezra had covered it with a tarp littered with bits of hay, thick dust and more spiderwebs than he could count.

Someone had pulled it out and polished it until it shone in the sunlight. Patches on the cloth seats revealed where mice had chewed holes through the fabric to make nests in the stuffing. Even without looking, he guessed the shafts had been repainted or replaced so they wouldn't snap the first time a horse was harnessed between them.

"What is this?" he asked.

His brothers chuckled, then Daniel said, "If you can't

recognize your own courting buggy, Ezra, then it's definitely been too long since you used it."

"I know what it *is*. I'm wondering why it's out here and polished up."

His brothers exchanged grins, and this time Jeremiah spoke. "After watching you mope around here recently—"

"I haven't been moping."

"After watching you *mope* around here recently," Jeremiah said again, "we talked it over."

"Talked what over?"

"We agreed that it's time for you to make a decision, big brother," Micah said, trying to look serious, but a smothered laugh escaped.

"A decision about what?"

"About Leah Beiler."

"What about her?"

"Don't play *dumm* with us," Amos said with a hearty chuckle. "We already know how she sets your brain to spinning like a top."

That he couldn't argue with. His judgment concerning Leah had been overwhelming his *gut* sense since before he began his *rumspringa*. In the ensuing years, that hadn't changed. So many things he wanted to say to her. Like how the sunshine glowed in her eyes, making them appear even a richer purple. Or how he liked the single curl that always escaped from beneath her *kapp* and teased him with the thought of her lush hair loose around her shoulders.

Micah laughed as he gave the buggy's bright blue plush velvet seat a quick swipe with a cloth and did the same to the slow-moving vehicle triangle on the back. "Maybe that's why he can't see what everyone else can."

Snapping the cloth toward Ezra, he laughed when his older brother jumped back. "You've never gotten Leah out of your head or out of your heart. It's time to stop waffling."

"Go and get cleaned up." Isaiah gave him a not-so-gentle shove toward the house. "No girl likes a man to smell like a barn when he comes a-courtin'."

Joshua reappeared, leading the buggy horse. "We'll have everything set for you by the time you get back. We'll take care of the milking for you this evening, so you don't have any excuse not to go."

"And if I don't want to go?"

His brothers laughed as if that question was the funniest thing they'd ever heard. When Isaiah told him to make sure he washed behind his ears—a warning their *mamm* had always given them before they left for Sunday services—he chuckled along with them.

When Ezra emerged from the house a short time later, his brothers crowed and clapped. They teased him about combing his hair and that he'd freshly shaved. Daniel bent over laughing when he pointed to Ezra's clean boots and unwrinkled light green shirt.

"Green like a frog," Daniel said before singing, "Froggie going a-courtin' and he did ride!"

"Uh-huh, uh-huh," Ezra's other brothers chimed in on the old folk song.

Ezra smiled in spite of his nerves. He appreciated his brothers' matchmaking, but he'd spent his time in the house trying to find a way to tell Leah why he was driving his courting buggy today. She hadn't admitted one of the reasons she had to be in Paradise Springs was to spend time with him. He had to hope that today he could prove to her that he was a real reason to stay.

As his brothers started in on another chorus of the long folk song about the courting frog, he didn't see what signal Joshua gave, but their younger brothers headed toward the house.

When they were out of earshot, Joshua said, "I pray it works out the way you want it to, Ezra. If we'd had any other choice, we wouldn't have forced the issue."

"Any other choice?" he repeated as he walked into the barn to retrieve a bucket and a small spade. Dropping the spade in the pail, he put them under the seat. He thought Joshua would ask why he was taking those items in his courting buggy, but he didn't.

When Joshua spoke, Ezra understood his brother's lack of curiosity. Joshua never liked delivering bad news, and he sighed before saying, "Amos and Isaiah told me that they heard Larry Nissley and Mervin Mast saying it's growing clear you're not really interested in Leah. Apparently both of them are."

His brothers often overheard idle talk from customers coming into their shops. On the farm, he had less chance to learn the latest gossip. Both Larry and Mervin were hardworking men, but he wasn't going to step aside so they could court Leah. Not until he and Leah had the talk he'd avoided for too long.

"*Danki*, Joshua," he said as he reached for the reins.

"Just so you know, Esther is having her work frolic today at the school for the scholars' parents. You might want to go there."

"I think I will." He slapped the reins gently on the horse and aimed its head toward the farm lane.

Joshua stepped back and waved as Ezra drove toward the road…and the conversation he couldn't delay any longer.

* * *

Leah paused as she swept the school's front porch. An open buggy was turning into the lane leading to the school. The scholars had left for the day, so why was someone coming now?

She smiled when she realized it was a courting buggy. Did Esther have a boyfriend? That he would come to the school made sense, because it would keep their courtship secret. With most of her brothers living at home, she might prefer not to have a suitor come to the house. The poor man would have to try to court her while surrounded by curious siblings.

Her mouth dropped open when she recognized the man driving toward her. Ezra! What was he doing with a courting buggy at the school? There was no reason to bring it for his sister. She could have borrowed it at home if she needed an open buggy for some reason.

He brought the buggy to a stop right in front of where Leah stood. Resting his arm on the back of the single seat, he smiled. He looked as fresh as a sunny morning with his neatly pressed green shirt. Again she couldn't help noticing how his suspenders emphasized his broad shoulders. He'd never been a scrawny kid, but he'd grown into a muscular man with his work on the farm.

Abruptly self-conscious, she tucked loose strands of her hair back under her *kapp*. She was dusty from helping Esther and the scholars and their *mamms* wash down desks and windows, as well as put supplies and books back in their proper places. Her apron was spotted with bright blue after one of the younger scholars had splashed paint on her while trying to help, and another had spilled milk on her sneakers, leaving them splotched with faint white stars.

"If you're looking for Esther, she's finishing up inside," Leah said, not quite meeting his eyes.

He leaned forward and rested his elbows on his knees. "I'm looking for you."

"Well, here I am." She went back to sweeping dust and bits of grass off the porch floor, hoping she appeared nonchalant even though her hands were clumsy as her fingers shook on the broom's handle.

"So you are." He jumped out and climbed the steps in a motion so smooth that it seemed as if he'd floated up to stand beside her. "Where's Mandy?"

"She headed home with the other scholars."

"Gut."

"Gut?" she repeated. When his eyes began to twinkle, she became more aware of how silly she sounded.

"Ja, because there isn't really room for three in the buggy." He leaned one hand on a porch upright and asked, "Leah Beiler, will you let me take you home?"

"Ezra, we're not youngsters, and this isn't a singing."

"Maybe not, but you need eventually to go home." He waved his straw hat at the school. "Unless you plan on sleeping in there tonight." Lowering his voice to a conspiratorial whisper, he added, "I can assure you that falling asleep with your head on a desk isn't very comfortable."

"That sounds like the voice of experience. Did you do that?"

"Only once."

"I don't remember that."

"It must have been the year before you started school. We'd had a particularly long game of softball at recess, and I ended up running around the bases a lot." His boyish grin resembled the mischievous one she recalled from

those long-ago innocent days. "The teacher woke me up and suggested I go splash cold water on my face. Everyone watched while I did."

"And teased you about it afterward."

His smile widened. "Of course. I was Easy-Asleep Ezra for the whole year."

"That's a mouthful of nickname."

"Which is probably why it was forgotten by the time school started the next fall." His expression grew serious again. "But we've gotten off the subject, Leah. Will you let me drive you home?"

"Are you sure that you can stay awake long enough?"

He gave a mock groan. "I should have known better than to tell you that story. You know enough about my misadventures already."

"And you know mine."

"Not all of them." He grew serious in spite of how his eyes sparkled. "I know the girl named Leah Beiler, but not the woman named Leah Beiler."

That betraying blush burned on her cheeks, and she half turned her back on him as she ran the broom along the last boards at the end of the porch. "There's not much difference."

"I disagree."

"Then you're wrong."

"Prove it to me."

At his challenge spoken in an utterly calm voice, she couldn't keep herself from looking back at him. The honest entreaty on his features defeated her protests even before she spoke another word.

Holding out his hand, he said, "Ride with me and prove me wrong."

She had to give him an answer. They couldn't spend

the rest of their lives in front of the school. Yet, to accept a ride in his courting buggy was certain to create a huge change in their relationship. It was one she wanted to take, but she wondered if she truly was being fair to Ezra.

Last night, Mandy had talked nonstop for almost an hour about what she wanted to do when they went back to Philadelphia. Leah thought she was talking about spending a few days in the city in addition to Isabella's sleepover until Mandy asked if they would be living in the same apartment or if they could move somewhere with room for a garden like her *grossmammi*'s.

He put his hand over hers on the broomstick. "Don't look serious," he said, his smile returning like the sun erupting past the edge of a cloud. "All I'm asking is if I can take you home."

"True." She drew her fingers out from beneath his and took the broom to the school's door. "Esther, do you mind if I leave now?"

Ezra's sister came to take the broom and smiled. "I'd say it's about time."

Leah decided the best answer to that was simply to bid the schoolteacher farewell. She hurried down the steps, as conscious of Ezra following close behind as if he were touching her.

He stepped past her and offered his hand again when he stood by the buggy. This time, she didn't hesitate, placing her fingers on his work-hardened palm. She wanted to keep holding his hand after he'd assisted her into the buggy but released it quickly. Even though there was only Esther to see them, she couldn't forget what remained between them. A thick wall built, brick by brick, by the decisions she'd made and the ones she must make.

Locking her fingers together on her lap, she watched

him come around the buggy. He glanced at her as he picked up the reins and said nothing, simply gave the horse the signal to go. When Esther waved, they did, too.

The horse stepped lively along the rise and fall of the road leading toward Paradise Springs. At a crossroads, he turned the horse in the opposite direction of their farms. It was a lovely spring afternoon, the perfect day for a drive. Yet…

"Is something wrong, Leah?" Ezra asked.

She almost said that feeling nervous with him was wrong, but the words wouldn't come out. Instead she said, "*Mamm* expects me home soon."

"I know, but she will be pleased by the reason for our little detour."

Curiosity replaced her uncertainty. "I won't ask you what you've got planned, because I learned long ago that it was useless when you want to tease me by knowing something I don't know."

He grinned. "I was right. You know me too well."

"But you've changed, too, Ezra."

"I have. For the better, I can assure you."

She nudged his arm with her elbow as he chuckled. His jesting set the tone for their conversation as they followed the twisting country road past farms and a new housing development for *Englischers*. The sound of hammers and heavy equipment was left behind when he steered the buggy onto a narrower road. Cars seldom came this way, but, if one did, there would scarcely be room for the buggy on the road, so Ezra pulled to the right as they approached the crown of every rise.

Relaxing, Leah drew in the lush scents of freshly cut hay and overturned earth. Winter had put the land to

sleep, but with spring, it and the creatures who lived upon it, including the farm families, had come back to life.

Ahead of them a few miles down the road, a covered bridge crossed a small stream. Its official name was Coblentz Mill Bridge, but Leah preferred what everyone called it: Toad Creek Bridge. The exterior of the wooden structure was painted a mossy green. Inside the wood was bare except for some boards advertising business that no longer existed. Reed's Drug Store had gone out of business before she was born, and the buggy shop's advertisement was for the one where her *grossdawdi* had bought her *daed*'s courting buggy.

The sound of the horse's hooves clattered hollowly as they drove inside the bridge. Sunlight found its way past every gap in the boards and through the triangular latticework near the roof, dappling them in sunshine and shadows. Seeing the pattern on the bridge's floor, she wondered if it had inspired the quilt pattern she enjoyed making.

"That's not *gut*," Ezra said as he pointed toward a decking board that had been painted a bright orange with the words *Danger—Weak Board* scrawled on the wall above it with an arrow aimed at the board.

"I hope it's fixed before it gets worse."

"Or someone puts a wheel through it." He moved the buggy farther to the left and urged the horse to hurry to the other side of the bridge before a car came in the other direction.

Ezra stopped the buggy past the stone walls edging the road beyond the covered bridge. He got out and lashed the reins to a nearby tree. Coming back to where she sat, he put his hand atop hers on the buggy's side. Late-afternoon birdsong filled the air along with the buzz of

bees working swiftly as they went from flower to flower in the bushes beside the road.

"When I passed here earlier in the spring, I saw some wild daffodils down along the stream," he said. "Your *mamm* mentioned to mine that she was hoping to find some to put in front of your porch. By now, they're long past blooming, so it's a *gut* time to transplant them. Shall we get some for her?"

"Ja," she said, pleased with the outing he'd planned.

He had her pull a metal pail out from under the seat. When she handed it to him, their fingers brushed, creating an actual spark. She knew it'd been caused by her shifting on the plush fabric of the seat, but each time they touched, she'd felt something like that bright flicker.

"This way," Ezra said, after helping her out of the buggy. He led the way past the stone wall and down to the stream.

On a level space close to the water, the brown and drooping stems of what once had been vibrant daffodils huddled among the grass. Ezra squatted down and began carefully cutting a circle in the dirt. He made it large enough so he could dig without disturbing the bulbs themselves.

Leah went to the stream and tilted the pail. Allowing a small amount of water to gather in the bottom, she carried it back to where he was working. He handed each clump of wizened stems to her as he lifted them from the ground. She placed the daffodils with dirt still around the bulbs and their roots on top of the water. Keeping the plants moist until they could be transplanted was vital for the daffodils to survive in their new home.

Working together with him, her fingers warmed by the soil, she released the last of the tension that she'd

carried with her since long before her return to Paradise Springs. She hummed lightly while she continued to take the plants and set them with care in the pail.

"You've got such a pretty singing voice," Ezra said. "I've always loved hearing you sing."

"I didn't know that."

"I never told you because I didn't want you getting such a swelled head your *kapp* wouldn't fit on any longer."

"Danki," she retorted. "That would have been embarrassing."

"See what a *gut* friend I am?"

She lowered another daffodil into the bucket. "Friend? Is that what we are?"

"That's what you told me you wanted the day of the mud sale. Is that what you still want?" His smile was gone, replaced by an intensity that captured her gaze and wouldn't let go. She saw how important her answer was to him.

Before she could answer him, she had a question of her own. Gripping the side of the metal bucket, she said, "The night before I left with Johnny, you and I were together alone. Do you remember it?"

"Ja." His voice was clipped, and she couldn't tell if he recalled that night with yearning as she did or if he remembered it only because it was the last time they'd seen each other for ten long years.

"We were talking, and you brushed a mosquito away from me."

"Ja."

"And we kissed. Was that kiss an accident because we both turned at the same time?" As soon as she spoke them, she wanted to pull back the words that she had

tried to leave unsaid since her return. She hadn't been able to submerge her curiosity, but would knowing the truth would be any easier?

"Ja."

With that single word, her heart plummeted into a deep pit of regret. For ten years, she'd dared to believe that night had been as special for him as it had been for her. For ten years, she'd been fooling herself.

She stood, too humiliated to stay. "I should—I should… that is, *Mamm* will be expecting me…" Words failed her entirely as tears flooded her throat.

He was on his feet and in front of her before she could take more than a pair of paces. She moved to step around him. He halted her by putting his hand on her left arm. She closed her eyes, unable to see what she feared was pity on his face.

His gentle fingers curved along her cheek. "Look at me, Leah."

"I can't. I shouldn't have said anything about something that happened long ago. I was being silly."

"You weren't being silly. Not then, and not today."

Slowly she opened her eyes and gazed up into his, which were the brown of the overturned earth behind her. For the first time since she had returned, she could read the emotions within them as easily as she once had. Suddenly her tears were for him and the grief he tried to keep hidden. Grief for those he had lost. His *daed*, Joshua's wife, Johnny…

And her?

She yearned to tell him that he had never lost her, that the connection they formed through their childhood had been one string she couldn't bear to let unravel. She had longed to return to her family because her home was

with them. She had longed to return to Ezra Stoltzfus, because her heart was with him.

"Ezra—"

"Let me finish, Leah. That kiss *was* an accident, but it's an accident that I have thanked God for every day since."

"You have?" The last of the frozen regret around her heart cracked and disappeared at his earnest words.

"Ja." His lopsided smile, the one she'd always liked best, tilted his lips. "I had wanted to show you how I felt, but I guess I was the coward your brother called me."

"You're not a coward. You've never been afraid to do what's right, even when it was difficult. And you're willing to take a risk to make your dream of making and selling cheese come true."

"But those things have never been as important as our friendship. I was afraid that by revealing the truth I'd ruin it. Especially if you didn't feel the same."

"I was afraid, too. Afraid that the kiss meant nothing."

He sighed and lowered his hand. "And why wouldn't you? I ran away like a frightened deer with the hunter on its tail. I felt bad that I hadn't taken you home properly, and I intended to tell you as soon as I was finished my chores the next evening, but you'd already left. I feared I had chased you away."

"No, you didn't. I didn't ever plan to leave Paradise Springs. I went with Johnny to bring him home."

"I know that now, but the kid I was then didn't."

She looked down at her clasped hands. "We make plans, but our plans must change when God has other plans for us."

"You make it sound as if God makes our choices and we have no free will to choose."

"We do have free will," she argued, astonished at his words. Had his faith suffered as much as her heart? "God allows us to make choices. But, like the loving *daed* He is, He wants to help us avoid the many potholes in the paths we walk. He may not hold our hands, but He's there if there's a rough patch we need help getting across."

"Even one that lasts for ten years?"

She nodded. "But that's in the past now."

"I don't want to be lost in the past any longer." His arm curved around her waist.

"Me, either." Her hands slid up to his shoulders as he brought her against his firm chest.

"Maybe last time it was an accident that I kissed you, but…" He lowered his mouth toward hers.

She held her breath, eager for another kiss like the one she'd dreamed about often. Then his lips found hers, and she lost herself, enthralled, in the moment that was even more glorious than she could have guessed. The last time they had kissed, they had been *kinder*. This time, they weren't.

And this time, she was kissing him back. How could she have thought that stolen kiss was perfection? It faded to nothing more than a pleasant memory as she savored kissing him.

He raised his mouth far enough so he could murmur, "As I was saying, the last time was an accident, but this time I definitely kissed you on purpose."

"I like on-purpose kisses." Happiness bubbled out of her in a giggle.

When he laughed, too, joy washed through her. *This* was what had been missing in her life. The sound of her laughter and his woven together into a single melody. Once it had been as familiar as her own heartbeat. When

she lost it, she lost a part of herself that left her drifting aimlessly through the years.

"I'll have to remember that." He gave her another kiss before he released her, his fingers lingering at her side as if he could not bear to let her go.

She understood that too well, because she already missed his arms around her. When she picked up the pail, her knees were unsteady. She took his hand as they walked back to the buggy. She had no idea how fleeting this happiness might be, because nothing had changed with Mandy's yearning to go back to the city, so she must enjoy every happy moment while she could.

Chapter Twelve

"Mandy? Where are you?" Leah called as she walked toward the barn that was a silhouette in the light from the setting sun.

When Ezra had dropped her off at the end of the lane after their ride, knowing that it was expected they would be discreet—in spite of his brothers' matchmaking—and not be seen in the courting buggy by her parents, she had decided to plant the daffodils right away as a surprise to *Mamm*. She knew Mandy would be eager to help, but where was her niece? She hoped the little girl hadn't gone across the field to Ezra's house again. It would soon be too late for Mandy to be out by herself.

At a sharp bark, she saw Shep come out of the house. Mandy was following at her top speed, but the little dog was leaving her farther behind with every step.

Leah stared as Shep rose to his hind legs, twirling about, his little paws bouncing in front of him. He dropped to the ground, barked again and repeated his dance.

The pail dropped from Leah's suddenly nerveless fingers. As Mandy reached her, she grasped her niece by the shoulders.

"Where's *Daed*?" she asked.

"I don't know. Shep—"

"I see him! We've got to find *Daed*. If—"

A scream came from the house.

Leah leaped over the pail as she raced to the back door. As she tore it open, *Mamm* cried out again from the front room.

One look was all Leah needed. *Daed* was face down on the floor, blood oozing beneath his head, his right arm twitching as if touched by an electric wire.

Whirling to Mandy who'd followed her in, she ordered, "Go to the barn and call 911 and have them send an ambulance right away. Can you do that?"

Her niece nodded, but kept staring at her unmoving *grossdawdi*.

"Go!" Leah grabbed her arm. "Tell them to come as fast as they can."

"Is he going to die?" Terror filled the little girl's voice, and Leah doubted her niece had heard a word that she'd said.

"Not if we get him help soon." Looking at *Mamm*, she said, "I'll call 911."

Unsure if *Mamm* had heard her, either, Leah ran outside with Shep at her heels. He kept barking, but didn't do his warning motions as she sped into the dusk-filled barn. She grabbed the flashlight that *Daed* kept on a shelf by the door.

For a second, her composure threatened to shatter as she wondered when or if *Daed* would ever use a flashlight again. It seemed impossible that less than an hour ago, she'd been in Ezra's arms, believing that everything was finally going in the right direction.

Pushing any thoughts but making the call from her

mind, Leah yanked an inner door open and sprayed light across the small room. Seeing the phone and its answering machine on a table under a dusty window, she shut the door so Shep's barking wouldn't drown out her voice. She picked up the phone and set the flashlight down as she listened for a dial tone, then called 911.

A woman answered almost at once, and Leah rapidly told her what they needed and their address. She answered the woman's questions about her *daed*'s condition, realizing how little she knew other than that he was senseless on the floor and that his right arm had been jerking about.

As soon as the woman said the ambulance was on its way, Leah thanked her and hung up. She reached for the flashlight, then froze as her eyes were caught by a familiar phone number on a yellowed pad of paper by the phone. It was the number for the phone they'd had in Johnny's apartment in Philadelphia. Written in *Daed*'s scrawling handwriting.

He had found their number and written it down. Why? Was he planning to call them? As old and brittle as the paper looked and as faded as the ink was, he must have jotted it down a long time ago. Yet, he'd never thrown it away. Why hadn't he called? Just once?

Blinking back tears, she reached for the latch. She had to return to the house. As she ran, she prayed God wouldn't take *Daed* today for many reasons.

Including him explaining why he'd written down their phone number and kept it.

The ambulance arrived within minutes, though it seemed like hours while Leah knelt by her unconscious *daed*'s side and kept up a steady patter to calm *Mamm*

and Mandy. Two young men came in, pulling a gurney stacked with equipment. She recognized them from the mud sale. That day, they'd been among the firefighters helping the *kinder* try on their heavy coats and helmets. Today, they were a blessing.

With a terse greeting, they motioned for Leah to move aside. She stood and watched as they opened up bags with their gear. Because she'd spent a lot of time at the hospital with Johnny, she knew what the equipment did. She answered the EMTs' questions and explained to her *mamm* what they were doing.

She drew Mandy close and felt the little girl shiver as if she were sick. Mandy's face was nearly as gray as *Daed*'s, and she choked back a soft cry of dismay when the emergency workers opened *Daed*'s shirt and placed on his chest and arms the small squares holding the electrodes that they hooked up to a portable machine with a readout on the front. Like Leah, the little girl was too familiar with equipment like an electrocardiogram.

"Shep needs you," she whispered to her niece. She hoped that the dog would distract Mandy at least a little bit from what was happening.

Mandy scooped up the dog, which was panting with its tongue drooping out of one side of its mouth. Shep expected to be praised for doing what he'd been trained to do, and the little girl complied, burying her face in his black fur and telling him what a *wunderbaar* dog he was.

The EMTs completed their examination quickly and with a minimum of conversation. One pulled out a cell phone. He pushed a single button. As soon as someone answered, he told the person that the unit was going to be transporting one man to the local hospital and listed the symptoms and test results they had.

Mandy moaned at the mention of a hospital and turned her face against Leah's side.

"It's *gut* that they're taking him where he can get the very best care," Leah said, stroking her hair. Mandy's *kapp* had fallen off at some point and lay, abandoned, beneath a chair that someone had moved aside.

"But the doctors at the hospital didn't save Daddy."

"I know." What else could she say? She was thankful that God had spared Mandy from being home the day Johnny died. In fact, neither of them had been in the apartment. It was a school day, and Leah had been grocery shopping, so her brother had died alone. She prayed again, as she had often, that her brother had let go of his anger and forgiven *Daed* and himself, allowing God into his heart before he breathed his last.

Leah was jerked back to the present when *Mamm* asked if she could ride to the hospital with *Daed*. The EMTs agreed, telling her that she must get in as soon as they had her husband on the gurney and loaded into the ambulance. They didn't want to delay getting *Daed* to the emergency room.

"I need my bonnet," *Mamm* said, looking dazed and uncertain.

Leah ran into the kitchen and snatched her *mamm*'s bonnet off the peg by the back door. Knowing that it would take at least a minute or two for the EMTs to load *Daed* into the ambulance, she put some cookies and lemonade in the cooler that Mandy carried to school. *Daed* loved snickerdoodles, and having them might offer him—and *Mamm*—some comfort at the impersonal hospital.

Rushing back into the front room, she handed the bonnet and the cooler to her *mamm*. *Mamm* nodded her thanks but said nothing as she followed *Daed*'s gurney

out of the house. Leah and Mandy went, too, but only as far as the porch.

Daed and the gurney were put quickly into the ambulance; then one EMT helped *Mamm* in, as well. In the moment before the doors were closed, Leah saw *Mamm* sit on an empty gurney beside the one where *Daed* was lying, motionless.

Mandy began crying, and Leah pulled her niece into her arms. During her short life, the poor *kind* had seen too much suffering. Mandy flinched when the ambulance driver switched on the emergency lights as the vehicle turned tightly in the yard and headed to the main road. She pressed her face to Leah's apron and moaned when the siren blasted at the same moment the ambulance reached the end of the lane.

Stroking her niece's hair, Leah watched the flashing lights and listened to the strident siren until both vanished. It was quick, because the vehicle was traveling fast. How long would it take for the ambulance to reach the hospital? It would be more than two hours by buggy.

"Let's go inside," Leah said.

"How will we know if *Grossdawdi* is okay?" Mandy asked.

"We can call."

Despair filled Mandy's voice. "My cell doesn't have any power. I used it to call Isabella when nobody was around. If I'd known we'd need it, I wouldn't have used it. I'm sorry, Aunt Leah."

"You don't need to apologize. And don't worry. We've got a telephone in the barn. That's where I went to call 911." She thought again about the phone number on the pad, then pushed it out of her mind. Ezra had been right earlier when he said it was time to stop being lost in the past.

"Where is it? I haven't seen it," she said, confirming Leah's hunch that Mandy had been so focused on her *grossdawdi* that she'd heard nothing Leah had said earlier.

"It's in a small room to the right of the stalls." Putting her hands on the little girl's shoulders, she turned her to look at the old barn, which was almost invisible in the thickening twilight. "See the wires coming from the road to the far corner of the barn? They are telephone lines."

"Why is there a phone in the barn? I didn't think Amish used phones."

"We don't use them in the house because we don't want our homes connected to the wider world. *Grossdawdi* had a phone installed in the barn in case he had to call the veterinarian if one of the cows got sick."

"What if you or Daddy or *Aenti* Martha got sick?"

She chuckled, amazed that she could when she'd just watched *Daed* leaving in an ambulance. "*Mamm* took care of us, except when your other aunt, *Aenti* Irene, broke her leg. *Aenti* Irene was taken to the clinic in the village." She looked up at the distant rumble of thunder. "Let's get inside before the storm comes."

"But don't we need to go to the barn and wait for the telephone to ring?"

"There is an answering machine, and..." She looked past her niece when she heard her name shouted.

Ezra ran along the farm lane. He didn't slow until he came up on the porch.

"I saw the ambulance," he said, panting from the run. "Who are they taking to the hospital?"

"*Daed*," she answered. "*Mamm* is riding with them."

"*Gut.* Abram will want her there with him. I'm glad I

called for Gerry's van before I came over here. He said he'd be here in a few minutes."

"You called him already?" The retired *Englischer* made his van available for trips that were too long for buggies.

"When the ambulance's lights and sirens came on, I knew someone was going to the hospital and that who-ever was here would want to get there as soon as pos-sible." Ezra looked over his shoulder as the sound of a powerful engine came from the far end of the farm lane. A long, white van turned in and drove toward the house. "There's Gerry now. Are you ready to go?"

"I will be in a minute." She didn't pause to thank him for his kindness. Instead, she rushed inside and called to Mandy to come with her. "Get your *kapp*. It's under the chair. I'll get our coats. We might be there late, and it's cold at night."

"No." Mandy halted in the middle of the front room and shook her head vehemently. "I'm not going."

"But I thought you'd want to see *Grossdawdi*—"

"No! Not if he's going to die like Daddy did."

He won't, Leah wanted to say. *He won't be alone as Johnny was.* She couldn't say that, not when the little girl was distraught already.

"Mandy—"

"Can you promise me that he won't die at the hospital?"

"No." She hated having to say that and almost cried when the little girl's face crumpled completely. Squat-ting, she looked directly into her niece's eyes. "Mandy, the number of our days is in God's hands. We must trust Him."

"But I love *Grossdawdi*."

"And he loves you, too. God knows that, but He sees

far beyond what we can. We have to believe that He wants only *gut* things for us."

"I'm scared."

"I know." She hugged her niece tightly so Mandy couldn't see her fear.

Ezra sat on the middle seat of the van and stared out the windshield at the lights of the passing cars. Gerry, his gray hair gleaming a sickish green in the lights from the dash, had turned on the radio to listen to the Phillies game. Though he usually followed the team, baseball was the last thing on Ezra's mind.

Beside him, Leah sat, her eyes aimed straight ahead, too. They'd left Mandy with *Mamm* and Esther, who promised to bring Deborah over to the house to keep Mandy company. Since they'd come back to the van, Leah hadn't spoken.

"Wie bischt?" he asked, speaking in *Deitsch* to keep their conversation private. He had no doubts that Gerry, after over five years of driving plain folks around, understood some of their language. He also knew that the driver wouldn't repeat anything he might understand.

"I am..." she replied in the same language. "I honestly don't know how I am. I'm scared. I'm hopeful. I'm grateful. I'm terrified."

He put his arm around her shoulders and slid her closer on the smooth seat. He was offering Leah comfort and companionship as she faced the unknown future. Under the circumstances, nobody would chide him for such behavior, even if Gerry mentioned it, which the *Englischer* wouldn't.

"I know," he said softly against the stiff material of her bonnet.

She didn't look at him. "And I feel sorry for Mandy. She's lost too much already, and she's just a little girl."

"Having someone you love become ill isn't easy at any age." He sighed. "When *Daed* died, I had to be strong for *Mamm*. Not that my brothers and sisters aren't strong, too, but the farm became my responsibility, along with making sure *Mamm* and my unmarried siblings were well taken care of."

"They have been blessed to have you." Finally she turned her head toward him, but he couldn't see her features in the dark van.

No problem. He could recreate every inch of her pretty face in his mind. After many years of practice, a time stretching back to before she left Paradise Springs, it was easy. He guessed her eyes were filled equally with worry and a determination to do everything possible to help her *daed*.

With a start, he realized he hadn't asked what had happened to Abram. He had been too focused on getting Leah to the hospital to be there for her parents.

"He falls down," Leah replied to his question. "I think he feels faint, but he refuses to talk about it."

"This has happened before?"

"*Ja*. At least twice since I got home. He suddenly collapses with no warning signs whatsoever."

He'd never imagined Abram, his strong and always reserved neighbor, being anything but as steady and unmoving as a stony ridge. Abruptly many things became clear. No wonder Leah had been hesitant, when Mandy was in school or with friends, to go even as far as the Stoltzfus Family Shops. She hadn't been trying to avoid him—she had wanted to remain at the farm in case her *daed* needed someone to call 911.

"*Danki* for coming with me," she whispered. "I don't know how I would have handled this long ride otherwise. Even God's patience might be tried when I keep praying the same words over and over for Him to let *Daed* live."

"Where else would I be?"

She shrugged beneath his arm.

Though he couldn't see her face, he put a single finger beneath her chin and tipped her face up so her mouth was close to his. He longed to kiss her again, to sweep away her fear and to think only of joy. Instead, he said, "If our situations were reversed, you'd be here for me."

"But I wasn't." Her voice broke on each word. "When you struggled after your *daed*'s death, I wasn't here for you."

"Because you were there for your brother. Even you, Leah, can't be in two places at once, and you were where you were supposed to be at that time. I had my family. Johnny and Mandy had only you."

"I wish I could have been here for you."

"I know you do, but you're here now."

The wrong thing to say, he realized, when she stiffened and pulled away. Was she thinking of returning to Philadelphia? After everything that had happened today? Her *daed*'s illness and the kisses by the creek? Defeat clutched his heart. If today's events wouldn't keep her in Paradise Springs, he had no idea what would.

Everything about the hospital emergency room was frantic and calm at the same time. Odors of cleaning fluid and disinfectants filled each breath Ezra took. He kept his hand on Leah's arm as they were directed to a counter to the left of the entrance. Around them swarmed emer-

gency personnel and the emergency room staff, along with families and patients seeking help.

A dark-haired woman who looked to be about the same age as his *mamm* stood behind the chest-high counter. Her name tag read Gloria. She looked up with a professionally kind smile when they halted in front of her.

"How may I help you?" Gloria asked.

"My *daed*—" Leah quickly corrected herself. "My father was brought here in an ambulance. Can you tell me where he is and how he's doing?"

"His name is Abraham Beiler," Ezra added.

Leah shot him a thankful smile, then turned back to the woman in the bright turquoise scrubs who was tapping the keys that must connect to the computer to her left. Leah might look composed, but her arm shivered in his hand. At every sound, she flinched and glanced around fearfully.

"Yes, Abraham Beiler," Gloria said, drawing his attention back to her. "He's waiting to see the neurologist. His wife is with him. Our policy is that ER patients can only have one visitor with them at a time." She glanced past Leah to him.

"Leah is his daughter," he said. "I'm a family friend." The words tasted bitter on his lips, but if she went back to the city, that would be all he'd ever be.

"If you'll take a seat in our waiting room, I'll let his nurse know you are here."

"Thank you," Leah whispered, her voice shaking.

Telling himself now wasn't the time to think about Leah's plans, Ezra steered her to where four rows of plastic chairs faced a television set. She sat on a red chair and stared up at the television. He glanced at it and

quickly away as cartoons flitted across the screen with the sound turned off.

"I hope we don't have to wait a long time," she said.

"It may be a while if the doctor is there now."

She wrapped her arms tightly around herself. He would have liked to put his arms around her, too, but the waiting room was filled with strangers. The doors opened and closed, spewing more people into the emergency room.

"A neurologist is a brain doctor," she said abruptly. "Why would *Daed* need to see a brain doctor?"

"Maybe," he replied, "they want to make sure Abram didn't get a concussion when he fell."

She nodded, clearly wanting to be comforted. "That makes sense."

Ezra stood when he saw two familiar faces near the door. Their bishop, Reuben Lapp, walked into the emergency room along with Isaiah. When they glanced around, he waved to them, and they hurried over.

"Reuben, Isaiah, *danki* for coming," he said.

The bishop nodded to him and sat beside Leah. He spoke quietly to her, and Ezra tried not to listen. The words of God's comfort and grace were for Leah. He longed for some of that grace for himself, that faith he'd once had that there was no problem too big for him and God to handle together.

Isaiah motioned toward a couple of open chairs against the opposite wall.

"Micah alerted us, and I contacted Reuben," he said without waiting for Ezra to say anything. "We got here as quickly as we could. How's Abram?"

Ezra sat beside his brother and told him the little he knew. Isaiah's brows lowered when Ezra spoke of how

this wasn't the first time Abram had fallen and how the family had kept his unsteadiness a secret at his request.

"Like *daed*, like son," Isaiah grumbled under his breath. "Both too proud to admit that they needed help."

"Fortunately Leah has been close to help both of them. Abram should be grateful that she knew what to do."

"She's here for now…unless you've convinced her to change her mind."

Ezra didn't bother to reply. His brother might think it was because Ezra didn't want to discuss his relationship with Leah…or Isaiah might sense the truth. Either way, there was nothing Ezra could say that wouldn't sound pitiful.

"Fannie!" Isaiah jumped to his feet and went to assist Leah's *mamm* to the chair he'd vacated.

Leah rushed across the room to hug her *mamm*. "How's *Daed*?"

"He wants to talk to you," Fannie replied. "Where's Mandy?"

"With *Mamm*," Ezra answered before Leah could.

"*Gut*. This is not place for a *kind* who's still mourning her *daed*'s death." She looked back at her daughter. "Go. Your *daed* is waiting to speak to you."

Leah took one step, then faltered. Ezra moved to her side and put his hand on her arm, not caring if everyone in the world was watching. "We'll wait here with Fannie. It'll be okay."

"Will it?" She was walking away before he could answer, even if he'd had an answer.

Leah heard moans of pain and hushed voices coming from behind the drawn curtains. Hospital staff went from room to room, comforting patients, drawing blood, run-

ning tests. She'd hoped she had become inured to suffering after the times she went to the ER with Johnny. She hadn't. She didn't think she ever could.

Repeating the prayer that Reuben had shared with her in the waiting room, she asked God to be with each of the sick or hurt people behind those curtains and with their families. *Give them hope, let them know that You are with them always, in the* gut *times and the bad.*

She stopped in front of the curtained door with the number four printed over it. Taking a deep breath, she drew the curtain back and stepped inside.

Daed was alone in the room, except for machines that beeped and listed numbers she had learned to read. A quick scan told her that her *daed*'s vitals were *gut*, though his pulse was elevated. That wasn't a surprise when he'd been brought by ambulance to the hospital.

He looked gray against the white sheets on the bed. The top was cranked up, so he had a view of the curtains without lifting his head. A bandage was wrapped around his forehead, and she guessed he'd cracked open the healing scab from his previous fall. She rushed to his bedside and clasped his left hand between hers, being careful not to jostle the needle hooked to the IV bag hanging behind him. If he pulled his hand away, too angry at her to let her offer him sympathy, then so be it. She loved him. She'd never stopped loving him, and she couldn't pretend otherwise so he wasn't upset.

But he didn't pull his hand away. Instead, he looked up at her with tear-filled eyes as he said, "*Danki*, Leah."

"I didn't do anything you need to thank me for, *Daed*."

"Your *mamm* told me how much you helped her when I…when I fell over. Neither of us is surprised, because

you have always helped those who need it, but we're both grateful."

"I'm glad I was there to call 911."

He grimaced as he pushed himself up to sit higher on the bed. Reaching behind him, she readjusted his pillow so it was comfortable. She started to step back, but *Daed* caught her hand, keeping her beside him.

"I'm glad you were there, too, Leah," he said in a gruff tone that she knew covered his emotions, "and not just to call the ambulance. I'm glad you are home."

"You are?" The words squeaked out before she could halt them.

He rubbed his forehead with his right hand, and she noticed how it quivered. She glanced up at the screen with his vitals listed on it. They remained the same.

"Don't look worried," *Daed* said. "The nurse told me that we'll have to get used to my hand shaking."

"Why? What's causing it?"

"I heard the nurses talking. They mentioned Parkinson's disease." He looked at his right hand. "I think it has to do with this shaking and maybe the falls, but they want the brain doctor to examine me so they can be sure. Will you stay here while he's here?"

"*Ja.*" She hid her surprise. "If you want me to. I'll get *Mamm*—"

He shook his head, then winced. "You know more about this *Englisch* medicine, so it'll be better if you explain it to her after the doctor's done. She'll get upset with the fancy words, but you'll understand them, won't you?"

"If I don't, I'll ask." She glanced up at the monitors again as she added in a faint whisper, "That's what I learned to do when Johnny was in the hospital."

"Leah…"

When her *daed* didn't continue, she looked back at him, fearful. He was regarding her steadily, his face revealing raw emotions that appeared as jumbled as she'd described hers to Ezra. How she wished Ezra was here! He was steady and calm and cared about her and *Daed*. To touch him would bolster her flagging strength.

"Ja, Daed?" she asked.

"It's time we talked."

"We are talking."

"But not about what's been bothering you. You don't understand why I sent your letters back unopened. I thought *you* would understand."

"I didn't, and I don't now." She took another deep breath, then added, *"Mamm* told me that you believed if Johnny and I had anything to say, we could say it to you directly."

"She's partly right."

"What's the other part?"

"I was ashamed that I had chased my own *kinder* away."

"You didn't chase Johnny away. He'd been planning to leave with Carleen for quite a while. It wasn't a spur-of-the-moment decision."

He stared up at the ceiling tiles where a water leak had made an abstract brown pattern. "Johnny would never have stayed here, even if we never had raised our voices to each other. He looked beyond our community from the moment he realized there were others who lived differently than we did. He was like a fire that burned too brightly and too fast. A fire that demanded more and more fuel to keep burning. A plain life would never have given him that endless supply of excitement and speed. I

knew as soon as he found work beyond Paradise Springs he would eventually be gone."

Compassion for her *daed* surged through her. "I know, but I never guessed he was jumping the fence that night."

"He had jumped it long before, though he remained beneath our roof." His eyes shifted toward the curtain, but whoever had paused beyond it kept walking. "He chose a wild gang to run about with."

"I wished he hadn't. They got into all kinds of mischief."

"I thought he might come to his senses when the Miller boy was killed in that car wreck, but he didn't."

"No," she said with a sigh, "but he did the right thing by trying to make a life with Carleen. He never could have guessed that she'd walk away from him and Mandy when the going got rough."

"But you didn't."

"How could I? They needed me. After his accident, Johnny couldn't care for Mandy by himself, and bringing her home would have been a worse blow to him than having Carleen leave. I couldn't separate Mandy from her *daed* or Johnny from his daughter."

"So you separated yourself from me."

Tears rolled out of her eyes and down her cheeks. "Don't think that I wasn't aware of that. I saw our phone number in the barn. Why didn't you call?"

"And say what? Johnny had made his decision, and so had you." He sighed. "I couldn't bring myself to throw that number away."

But he couldn't call and beg. As *Mamm* had told her, *Daed* was a proud man who struggled to be humble.

"In his own way," Leah said, "I think Johnny missed home, too."

Surprise widened her *daed*'s eyes before sadness dimmed them. "*Danki* for telling me that. And let me be as honest with you. During those quarrels with Johnny, when I knew I was losing him, I never guessed you would go, too. That's why I sent back your letters unread. I hoped you'd come home to find out why."

Leah's breath caught at her *daed*'s grief. All the homesickness she'd suffered, all the frustration she'd endured when every one of her letters came back, the pain of believing that she wasn't missed... Every bit of it vanished as she saw the truth on her *daed*'s face. For every hour she had regretted not being home, he'd regretted not having her there.

"And, Leah, I don't know if I could lose you again."

"I know." She leaned her head against his chest so he couldn't see her face. As she listened to his steady heartbeat, she knew that, somehow, she had to convince Mandy to stay. Not out of guilt, because that might lead to her niece becoming as resentful as Johnny had been.

But somehow...

Chapter Thirteen

If he weren't a farmer, Ezra decided he might like to run a general store like Amos did. Everything had a sense of order about it, as did the fields on the farm once the crops were planted. The shelves were set in the two rows that ran the depth of the store. Cans and bottles and boxes and bags were stacked on the shelves to the ceiling. A long-handled gripper hung at the end of each row so that shoppers could get down items from the higher shelves without resorting to using a step stool. He'd been fascinated by them as a boy and excited the first time *Mamm* let him wield it.

Fresh meat and vegetables lent an interesting aroma to the store. Ground coffee and fruits sweetened the air and made his stomach growl despite the large dinner he'd eaten at midday.

Supper would be on the table by the time he got back from coming into Paradise Springs to get more baling twine for tomorrow, if *Mamm Millich* didn't go into labor. She was restless, so her time was coming soon, but he figured he could take a quick drive into the village as the sun was setting. He knew the baling twine was shelved

at the back of the store with the other nonfood items that Amos sold. He'd grab it and get out so Amos could close up. The parking lot in front had been deserted when Ezra drove the family's buggy up to the store, so he'd be the last customer of the day.

He walked past the black potbellied stove that was cool now that the days were warm. He'd reached the end of the row of shelves when he heard "…and three yards of the red cotton, if you have it, Amos."

Leah!

Ezra's heart lurched. He hadn't seen her for the past week because she'd been busy with helping her parents adjust to what life would now be like since Abram's diagnosis of Parkinson's disease. Though he could have gone across the field to visit as *Mamm* had, he had resisted. He told anyone who asked—and his brothers did frequently—that he needed to remain close to the farm to be there when the calf was born. That was the truth, but only part of it.

He was tired of the hurting whenever he thought of how, once Abram was stabilized and accustomed to his new limitations, Leah might accept the invitation to go to Philadelphia. After her last visit to the Beilers' house, *Mamm* had sadly mentioned that Mandy talked of little but her plans to go to her best friend's birthday party. Leah would never allow the little girl to make that journey alone.

"I've got three yards, Leah," his brother said, "but the bolt is almost gone. If you want to take the last couple of yards, I can give you a really *gut* price for it."

"*Danki*, Amos. I'm sure I can find a use for it." There was a lilt in her voice that he hadn't heard since her return to Paradise Springs. It took him instantly back in time to

the day so many years ago when they'd gone fishing by the creek that cut between their farms and she'd hooked the biggest trout ever caught out of the rapidly running spring waters. That was the day when, as he listened to her joyous laugh, he'd begun to realize that he wanted to be more than her friend.

"You or your students will, I'm sure."

His brother's easy words stabbed at Ezra's heart. Students? She must have made her decision to return to the city. Blinded with pain, he started to turn to leave, but his shoulder bumped a stack of cans at the end of the row. They crashed to the concrete floor and rolled in every possible direction.

"Couldn't you just say *hi*, big brother?" Amos asked with a chuckle as he came around the fabric counter and began gathering up the cans. "No need for a grand entrance."

Ezra gave a terse laugh as he picked up the cans, too, and put them on the counter beside the bolt of cloth. Leah collected the ones that had rolled toward her and set them beside his.

As Amos chased after a couple of cans that had bounced farther away, Ezra couldn't go without saying something to Leah. Again she spoke before he could come up with something that didn't sound *dumm*.

"I needed some fabric," she said, "and your brother sells the perfect cottons and blends for quilts. He has already sold the quilts I brought home with me."

"I need more of Leah's handiwork." Amos chuckled as he returned with the last of the cans. "Last weekend, two customers got into an argument over which one had seen her remaining quilt first, and they were snarling like two cats. I put an end to the quarrel by taking the sec-

ond woman's name and phone number. I told her that I would call her as soon as Leah brought in another quilt, so she could have the first chance to see and purchase it."

An appealing flush warmed Leah's cheeks, and it took all of Ezra's willpower to keep from running his fingertip along that soft pink, inviting her to turn her lovely eyes toward him. Would a man ever tire of losing himself in their warm, purple depths?

"That's great," he said.

If either Leah or his brother noticed how abrupt his answer was, he saw no sign. Amos quickly wrapped the fabric so it wouldn't get dirty on the way home, and she paid him, thanking him again for the discount he'd given her.

As she walked toward the front of the store, Amos asked, "Why are you standing here, Ezra?"

"I need some baling twine."

"You *need* to stop letting Leah walk away from you. One of these days, she's going to keep going."

"She may keep going whether I go after her or not."

Amos's brows arced at the unmitigated resentment in Ezra's voice. Grabbing a roll of baling twine, he shoved it across the counter. "Pay me later. Go after her now while you still have a chance. Set aside your pride and persuade her to stay here. While you can!"

Ezra nodded. Again his brother was right. His pride had been wounded when she had gone without warning, and he had lived the past ten years on the edge of the community. Part of it, but not really. That he'd been unhappy and alone should have been a lesson for him in how worthless pride was, but he clung to its tatters as if they were a lifeline. He had to find a way to let them go.

For *gut*.

For Leah.

He wasn't sure, but as he rushed to his buggy, he thought he heard Amos's satisfied laugh. He looked back to see his brother turning the closed sign forward on the store's door and giving him a thumbs-up.

It didn't take long for Ezra to catch up with Leah, who was walking along the side of the road, her bare feet kicking up dust with every step. She edged off the road as he approached, and she didn't look back to see who was coming toward her in the thickening twilight.

He slowed the buggy to match her pace and called out, "Don't you know it's dangerous to walk along these roads at dusk? Would you like a ride?"

She looked at him, and there was enough light for him to see her conflicting emotions. Unlike in Amos's store, she didn't hide her true feelings behind a mask of cheery goodwill.

"Danki," she said, placing the bolt of fabric in the back with the baling twine.

As soon as she was sitting beside him, he gave the horse the order to go. "How's Abram now that he's home?"

"Ornery."

"Meaning that he's back to normal?"

She chuckled, and he saw she was astonished at her own reaction to his question. *"Ja.* He doesn't like having to take the medicine the doctors gave him, but I think Dr. Vandross, his neurologist, impressed on *Daed* its importance when he released *Daed* from the hospital."

"How did he get past your *daed*'s stubbornness?"

"He told *Daed* that there's no cure for his Parkinson's, but that if he wants to slow its progress, *Daed* needs to take his pills at the right time every day."

"And I'm certain you're making sure he does."

"At first. Now that *Mamm* understands his prescriptions and what they do, she's taken over scolding him if he forgets." A wispy smile warmed her soft lips. "That's the way it should be, and *Mamm* is enjoying having a chance to take care of him the way she's wanted to." She focused on her hands, which were folded in her lap. "Ezra, *Daed* explained to me why he returned my letters."

As the sun headed toward the horizon where clouds were rising up to claim more and more of the sky, he listened while Leah poured out what Abram had told her in the emergency room. She didn't spare either herself or her *daed* from blame for the years they'd been apart, but the happy lilt returned to her voice as she spoke of how they were trying to mend what they'd almost lost forever.

That's letting go of pride. The muted voice came from his own conscience. *Being willing to assume responsibility for your mistakes and not dwelling on your accomplishments.*

Was he willing to do that? As he turned the buggy onto the lane leading to her house, he thought of how he'd kissed Leah the night before she left, then run away like Georgie Porgie in the nursery rhyme he'd learned from *Englisch* friends. When she went away, he could have gone after her, telling her that he loved her. She'd come home, and still he'd kept his feelings to himself. Another mistake? How many more would he make before he was willing to acknowledge them? First to himself and then to her.

And to God. How could he tell Him that he had let foolish pride guide his life instead of heeding the truth?

All you need to do is trust in Him. That voice, so soft he easily could have missed it as he struggled with him-

self, came from a place far deeper than his own conscience. It came from his heart.

Was it that easy?

He drew the buggy to a halt in front of the Beiler house and turned to look at Leah. Really look at her. Not just her pretty face, but her generous heart.

"*Danki* for the ride, Ezra."

"Don't go yet. There's something I want to talk to you about."

"Is something wrong?"

"I'd say it's the opposite. For the first time in a long time, something may be completely right."

"I don't understand."

He put his hands around hers and drew them and her closer to him. "I've been living my life for the future. Not for now. Always talking about the things I dreamed I'd do someday. Never about the things I should be thinking about now. About being a better brother, a better son, a better friend—"

"You have always been a *gut* friend. The best I've ever had."

"About being a better man in God's eyes." He released her hands and framed her face gently, taking care not to knock her bonnet awry. Easily he could lose himself in her *wunderbaar* eyes that glowed in the last light of the day. "About being a better man in your eyes, Leah."

"I don't know a better man than you." She ran her fingers lightly along his cheek and over the whiskery line of his jaw.

He longed to lean into her touch, but he couldn't put off what he needed to say. Not again, when she must have been talking to Amos about teaching a quilting class. Why else would his brother have mentioned her students?

"When I said things were going right," he began, "you said you don't understand. Don't you see? Everything changed the day I asked you to ride with me to collect daffodil bulbs for your *mamm*, and I kissed you."

Her cheeks grew warm beneath his hands, and he smiled at how she was blushing, though he couldn't see clearly as the twilight erased the color from everything.

"Asking you to ride with me and kissing you," he continued, "were the best decisions I've made in a very, very long time. Not only because I started listening to my heart, but I started listening for God again." He brushed his lips against hers.

She gasped with soft delight, then whispered, "I didn't know you stopped listening to Him." She raised her eyes to meet his gaze.

His loving gaze, he hoped. *God, let her see what is truly in my heart, for words can't explain fully how much I love her.*

"Because my life was empty after you left," he said, "I tried to fill myself up with other matters." His thumb traced her high cheekbone. "Who would have guessed that God would bring you home, and you could show me that having only a partial faith may be worse than having none? If I hold that God is almighty, then I need to believe, too, that His ways are a marvel to behold. I need to accept that I may be blind to His plan, but everything that happens is part of that plan." He put two fingers beneath her chin and tilted it gently toward him. "That *you* may be part of the plan."

"I know you're part of what He intends for me."

"Only if you stay here in Paradise Springs, Leah. Let me ask you what I've been wanting to ask you for weeks. Will you stay here, or do you intend to leave again?"

* * *

At his question, Leah pulled back from Ezra as far as she could. She longed for his arms around her, because his touch made her head spin and her heart dance. The answer should be easy when she loved him. But it wasn't.

"You're asking for me to choose between you and Mandy," she whispered.

"No. I'm asking you to choose between living in Philadelphia and living here."

He made it sound simple, and when she was with him, it was. Deciding became complicated when she heard Mandy speak of home and knew her niece was speaking of the city.

Quietly she said, "I've spent the past decade trying to make sure Mandy didn't feel deprived because her *mamm* abandoned her and her *daed* was an invalid. Mandy and Johnny were my whole life. Everything I did, every choice I made, everything I struggled for was for them."

"Nobody denies that you've given every bit of yourself to them. You didn't stop after Johnny died. You returned, ready to atone for sins that were never yours, because here you could give your niece the home and family you wanted her to have."

"Ja."

"But now she wants to go back to the city, and you have to wonder if everything you did was for nothing."

"No!" She sat straighter. "It wasn't for nothing! I've raised her to know love and to know God. She's a *gut* girl who gives love easily and believes everything always works out for the best."

He folded her hand between his. "And what will work out best for her, Leah?"

Again the answer should have come readily to her lips.

Again it didn't. Tears filled her throat and burned in her eyes. "I don't know any longer. I do know that I want her to be happy as her *daed* never was."

"And if she can only be happy returning to Philadelphia and living with her *Englisch* friend?"

She blinked swiftly, trying to hold back her tears. "If I want her to be truly happy, I must be willing to let her go back to Philadelphia."

"Alone?"

"My home is and always has been here." She pulled her hands out of his and pressed them to her face. "I pray I have enough strength to let her go if that is what she needs."

"You are the strongest person I know." He drew her hands down and sandwiched them between his.

"I feel weak and helpless. Can I depend on you to be here to help me remain strong, Ezra?"

"You can depend on me for anything." His voice deepened to a rumble as he cupped her chin gently again. "And everything."

"Leah! *Komm!* Now!" The shout came from the house. Looking past Ezra, she saw *Mamm* waving from the kitchen door. She jumped out of the buggy and ran to the open kitchen door. She heard Ezra's boots pounding behind her.

"Was iss letz?" he shouted at the same time as Leah asked the same question in *Englisch*, "What's wrong?"

"Mandy is gone."

"Gone?" Leah's happiness and hope in the wake of her conversation with Ezra shattered. "Where?"

Mamm wrung her hands in her apron. "It's my fault. She got to talking about going to that Isabella's party, and I said it might not be possible for her to go."

"Oh, *Mamm*," she moaned. "She's had her heart set on going."

"But she's an Amish girl, and she doesn't belong in Philadelphia."

Daed came to the door. Drawing *Mamm* gently aside, he motioned for Leah and Ezra to enter.

"Fannie," he said as they gathered near the kitchen table, "as much as we wish it to be true and as *gut* a job as Leah has done in raising her to live a plain life, she is both Amish and *Englisch*."

Mamm dropped into her chair and began to cry. "I know. I know. It's that I can't bear to lose another one of you. First Johnny and Leah. Then I almost lost you, Abram."

He sat beside her and put his arms around her shoulders. Leah tried not to gasp, but she'd never seen *Daed* show this much affection for her *mamm*. That he did was both a sign that his health scare was changing him and also how fearful he was for Mandy.

"You haven't lost me, and we'll find Mandy." He raised his eyes to Ezra. "Will you help?"

"Ja," he said, and she knew what he'd told her was true. She *could* depend on him for anything. "Do you have any idea where she was headed?"

"Philadelphia, I'm sure." *Mamm* moaned and hid her face in her hands. "She's a city girl."

"Which is *gut* because she knows how to deal with traffic," Leah said.

"But she doesn't know anything about the dangers out here in the country."

Daed pushed himself to his feet and wobbled for a moment. He waved Leah away as she reached to steady

him. Stepping past her, he opened the kitchen drawer and looked inside. "She took a flashlight."

"Thank God for that," Leah said as she grabbed the other flashlight. Checking that it worked, she added, "If she has turned it on, we'll be able to see her, and so will anyone else who passes her. Maybe we can catch her before she reaches Route 30."

"No, no." *Mamm* rocked back and forth with her despair. "They drive so fast on that road."

Leah blinked back tears as she couldn't help but wonder if *Mamm* had reacted just like this the night she and Johnny left. She longed to hug her and apologize for causing her *mamm* such despair. Instead, she looked at Ezra and yanked open the door. "The quickest way to Route 30 is across your farm, Ezra."

"Let's go. We'll stop at the house and get my brothers to join the search." He held out his hand, and she clutched it. As her fingers shook in his, she half expected her *daed* to chide her for being bold.

Instead *Daed* said, "I will go and—"

"*You* will sit there," *Mamm* said in a tone Leah had never heard her use with her husband. "Let them go and alert the neighbors."

"But—"

"Sit there!"

"*Ja*," *Daed* said as he sank back into the chair.

Leah was unsure if her *daed* would remain compliant once they'd left. She prayed that, for once, he would heed *gut* sense and not be mulish. Holding Ezra's hand, she hurried with him into the field separating the two farms. She wanted to go faster but had no idea how long it would take to find the little girl. If they ran now, they could tire themselves out before they found Mandy.

Where was she? *Mamm* was right. Mandy didn't know enough about the countryside to recognize the dangers she could face being outside as night fell.

Her steps faltered as she heard Shep's distinctive yip-yip and a coyote's howl. She hadn't seen Shep in the kitchen. Mandy must have taken the dog with her. Had she put him on a leash? If he decided to chase after a feral dog, he could be killed.

Wishing for more light than the flashlight she carried, she looked skyward. Light outlined a bank of clouds. The moon should emerge from behind them soon. They could use every bit of its dim light.

She froze when she heard a scream.

Mandy!

Ezra seized her arm to halt her as she started to run in the direction of the scream. Was he out of his mind?

"Let me go! That's Mandy!" she cried. "She's in trouble."

Suddenly from out of the darkness, Shep began barking in a frantic tone he'd used only once before. It had been when a dog came too fast and too close toward Mandy. He'd been determined to protect her then.

Now...

Snatching the flashlight out of her hand, Ezra aimed it ahead of them. The small circle of light revealed an astounding sight. A few yards away, Mandy squatted with her arms protectively stretched out in an attempt to guard a cow that was lying on the ground. A low growl came from the far side of the cow, who let out a frantic moo. Was that Shep?

No, she realized with horror as the growling animal shifted. Two eyes glittered malevolently in the night. Not Shep's, because the eyes were too high off the ground.

It was a lanky coydog, ready to attack.

"Scream!" Ezra ordered. "As loud as you can. We have to scare it away!"

She did, scraping her throat with her shrill cries. As she took a breath, she heard Mandy shriek again.

Ezra ran forward, keeping his flashlight focused on the coydog's matted fur. Reaching Mandy, he grabbed her flashlight and aimed both at the beast. Shep continued barking wildly as they screamed and yelled.

More shouts came from the far side of the field. Lights bounced as Ezra's brothers ran toward them.

The coydog growled once more, then, realizing it couldn't fight so many enemies at once, it spun about and fled toward the trees edging the creek.

Leah dropped to her knees and pulled Mandy to her. "Are you hurt?"

"I'm fine." She caught Shep before he could race after the coydog. "We're fine. Me and Shep and *Mamm Millich* and her baby."

"Mamm Millich!" Ezra ran around to the other side of the cow and began to examine her and the tiny calf lying against her side. "What's she doing out here?"

"I don't know." Mandy stroked the cow's side.

"Thank the *gut* Lord that you came this way. If you'd taken the other road to reach the highway leading back to Philadelphia—"

"Why would we go that way? Shep and I were coming to see if the calf had been born. As we crossed the field, we heard her mooing. Then we saw that awful coyote creature sneaking toward her. We tried to protect her, but it kept coming closer."

Ezra reached across the cow to put a hand on Mandy's shoulder. "You did a *gut* job. You probably saved her life."

"But how did she get out here?" Leah asked, coming to her feet.

"When I checked her before going to the store, she was very restless. Pacing in the stall. If she bumped the door just right, she might have been able to pop the latch. Once it opened, she went in search of the rest of the milk herd. Somehow she got turned around and came into this field."

His brothers encircled them and peppered them with questions. As soon as they heard about the coydog, Daniel and Micah ran back to the house. They might have a chance to kill it before it tried to attack another of the animals on the farm.

Ezra sent Joshua to check that the rest of the herd in the pasture was unharmed, and Leah asked Jeremiah to let her parents know that Mandy and Shep had been found and were safe.

As the two brothers went in opposite directions, Ezra handed the two flashlights to Leah. She gave one to Mandy as he gathered the newborn calf up in his arms. It squirmed and bawled until his gentle voice calmed it. *Mamm Millich* heaved herself to her feet, not wanting to be separated from her baby. When Ezra looked over his shoulder, Leah smiled and motioned for him to lead the way back to the barn. She and Mandy walked on either side of *Mamm Millich*, carefully guiding the cow across the field.

An hour later, the excitement was over. *Mamm Millich* and her calf were back in the stall, where Ezra had wired the latch shut to avoid another escape. His youngest brothers had returned to report that, though they had seen paw prints, the darkness had prevented them from tracking the coydog. The herd was brought in as they would be every night until the coydog was no longer a threat.

Mandy and Shep were declared heroes. Mandy enjoyed cookies and a glass of cold milk while Shep lapped from a bowl of milk in the barn. They admired the new calf, which was already steady on its feet and nursing greedily.

"Auntie Leah?" asked Mandy as she wiped cookie crumbs off her apron. Shep hurried to eat them the second they hit the floor. "Why did you ask about me going back to Philadelphia tonight?"

Leah glanced at Ezra. He gave her the special smile he reserved for her. The sight of it gave her the courage to say, "That is where we feared you were going when *Mamm* and *Daed* couldn't find you."

"I left them a note. I told you, Leah, that I wouldn't leave the farm without letting you know where I was going."

"Where did you put it?"

"In the front room."

"They were busy preparing supper in the kitchen, and they probably never went into the front room." Putting her arm around Mandy's slender shoulders, she said, "They thought you were trying to get to Philadelphia because your *grossmammi* said you probably wouldn't be going to Isabella's party. She thought you were angry enough to run away."

"I wouldn't do that." Tears welled up in her eyes. "I've seen what Daddy's leaving did to you. I would never sneak away like that."

"But you want to go to Isabella's party?"

"I do."

"Do you want to stay there? You call Philadelphia home, and I know you're finding life here strange."

"I don't know, but I want to go back at least once to be certain."

Leah hugged her niece. "That's fair. I will talk to your grandparents, and we'll see about arranging for you to go to Isabella's party. Once you come back here, we'll talk, and you can decide if you want to go back or stay here."

"What if I want to leave later?"

"We'll take each day as it comes."

Ezra walked to them as he said, "'This is the day which the Lord hath made, we will rejoice and be glad in it.' And we will be glad, Mandy, for each day you spend with us. But there is one day when you must be here."

"When?"

Looking over the little girl's head, he smiled at Leah. "The day when your *aenti* marries me."

As Mandy squealed with excitement and Shep twirled around with her, Leah stepped around them to stand face-to-face with Ezra. "You want to marry me?"

"It's what a man does when he loves a woman. *Ich liebe dich*, Leah. Can I dare to believe that, in spite of my foolishness for the past ten years, you might love me, too?"

"Ja. Ich liebe dich." She put her arms around his shoulders as he drew her to him.

"Will you marry me?"

In the moment before his lips found hers, she whispered a single word that she meant with all her heart. *"Ja."*

Epilogue

"And this is *Mamm Millich* and *Boppli Millich*." Mandy's voice became more excited as she added, "They're the cows I told you about. The ones Shep and I saved from the coyote."

"Wow!" Isabella Martinez stood on the bottom rail and leaned over the fence as Mandy did. The two girls were close to the same size. One wore plain clothing, and the other was dressed in jeans and a garish T-shirt with the logo of a band Leah had never heard of.

Leah folded her arms on the top of the fence. "Did you tell Isabella that the cheese she tried earlier came from *Mamm Millich*'s milk?"

"Really?" Isabella jumped down from the fence. "Mandy, you're right. Everything about being on a farm is cool. I hope I can visit again."

"Whenever you wish," Leah said with a smile.

It was easy to smile now. After Mandy had gone to Isabella's sleepover, she had returned to Paradise Springs, saying Philadelphia was too loud and dirty and there weren't any cows or any of *Grossmammi*'s snitz pie or Esther's cookies. She'd missed her family and Shep and

the friends she'd made at school. She wanted to stay on the farm. At least for now, because, though she'd decided she didn't want to be a nurse after being sickened by the sight of the blood after her *grossdawdi* fell in the front room, she now was talking about becoming a veterinarian. Leah guessed her niece's career plans would change many times before she completed eighth grade.

In addition, even though *Daed* had cranky days and sometimes refused to admit there was any way but his, he seemed resolved to savor every hour he had with his family. Leah had found herself laughing with him as they hadn't for several years before she and Johnny left.

"Ah, here are my favorite girls." Ezra walked toward them, carrying an armload of sweet corn. "See what I found in the garden?"

As Leah listened to the girls giggle in excitement, she smiled at Ezra. He was the main reason she found it easy to smile now. They planned to marry as soon as the harvest was over and the late fall wedding season began.

He gave the corn to the girls and told them to take it home so *Mamm* could cook it for them for lunch. As they ran away, giggling, he held his hand out.

Leah put hers in it. Neither of them spoke as they strolled after the girls. With him, she was truly home.

* * * * *

Dear Reader,

I am excited to write the Amish Hearts series. It is set in Lancaster County because I like to visit Amish country to stock up on pies—whoopie and shoofly. Going there gives me the feeling of coming home when I see the houses, barns and silos of the farms. I grew up on a farm outside a teeny town in northern New York. We spent summers barefoot helping in the garden. One of my first "outside" chores was feeding the chickens and collecting eggs. There still are local auctions to raise money for volunteer fire departments. I'm glad you chose to spend time with the Stoltzfus family—along with some of my special memories—in Paradise Springs.

Stop in and visit me at joannbrownbooks.com. Look for my next book in the Amish Hearts series coming soon from Love Inspired.

Wishing you many blessings,
Jo Ann Brown

COMING NEXT MONTH FROM
Love Inspired®

Available January 19, 2016

A DADDY FOR HER TRIPLETS
Lone Star Cowboy League • by Deb Kastner

Clint Daniels is a mountain man who needs nothing and no one. But helping widow Olivia Barlow and her six-year-old triplets with her small horse farm could be his chance to become a husband and father.

A HUSBAND FOR MARI
The Amish Matchmaker • by Emma Miller

Single mom Mari Troyer never thought she'd return to the Amish life—or that she'd find love. With her little boy playing matchmaker with carpenter James Hostetler, Mari might just be ready to make her stay permanent.

THE TEXAS RANCHER'S RETURN
Blue Thorn Ranch • by Allie Pleiter

Rancher Gunner Buckton suspects single mom Brooke Calder is at Blue Thorn Ranch to persuade him into signing away rights to the creek on his land. Can he learn to trust the pretty widow and see they're meant to be together?

A SOLDIER'S VALENTINE
Maple Springs • by Jenna Mindel

Retired army captain Zach Zelinsky wants a quiet life selling his artwork. But when the tea shop owner next door, Ginger Carleton, insists they enter the Valentine's Day window-display competition together, he'll find what he's been missing: love.

THE HERO'S SWEETHEART
Eagle Point Emergency • by Cheryl Wyatt

Returning home to care for his ill father and their family diner, military medic Jack Sullenberger clashes with spirited waitress Olivia Abbott. As they work together to save the restaurant, they'll discover they have more at stake...their happily-ever-after.

HIS SECRET CHILD
Rescue River • by Lee Tobin McClain

A snowstorm strands Fern Easton and her four-year-old foster daughter at a dog rescue farm with her friend's brother. Could finding out Carlo Camden is her little girl's real father destroy everything or be Fern's chance for a forever family?

LOOK FOR THESE AND OTHER LOVE INSPIRED BOOKS WHEREVER BOOKS ARE SOLD, INCLUDING MOST BOOKSTORES, SUPERMARKETS, DISCOUNT STORES AND DRUGSTORES.

LICNM0116

REQUEST YOUR FREE BOOKS!

2 FREE INSPIRATIONAL NOVELS
PLUS 2
FREE
MYSTERY GIFTS

Love Inspired®

LII5